Additional praise for Ben L
STORIES FOR NIGHTTIME AND SO̶M̶ ̶ ̶ ̶ ̶ ̶ ̶ ̶ THE DAY

"Some write like a dream, but each of these impressive stories reads like one (even those written 'for day'). Disarmingly simple and startlingly profound, Ben Loory's tales take readers through a wholly original universe of whimsy and pathos, moral darkness and brilliantly illuminated truths. Like the best dreams, they resonate, linger and haunt long after the Ambien wears off."

—JAMES P. OTHMER, AUTHOR OF *THE FUTURIST*

"Quite unlike anything else I have read, a singular work that seems content to explore a universe all its own, in the manner of, say, 'Kubla Khan' or *The Circus of Dr. Lao*. The cumulative effect is not cloying but strangely exhilarating, both for its deadpan considerations of life and death and the things that happen in between, and for some unexpected revelations about the essence of storytelling that arise from its stripped-down style. It will be exciting to see what this quietly fearless writer publishes next."

—DENNIS ETCHISON, AUTHOR OF *THE DARK COUNTRY*

"Ben Loory is a writer who makes me feel less alone in the world. He also makes me feel like the world is more—and not less—absurd than I had originally suspected, which always comes as a strange relief. All of this is another way of saying that Loory is an original, and a good one, and someone well worth reading. Funny, weird, insightful, and wry. A giver of wincing laughter. I recommend him highly and could easily see several cults forming around his work. Good cults, too. Not the staid, mediocre variety."

—BRAD LISTI, AUTHOR OF *ATTENTION. DEFICIT. DISORDER.*

"Ben Loory is a master cosmologist waiting to be discovered, with a parabolic telescope that will allow you to see right to the living heart, not of the matter, but of matter itself, of what matters."

—ANDREW RAMER, AUTHOR OF *Little Pictures: Fiction for a New Age*

"Ben Loory's stories are small surprises of beauty and wonder—often tragic, sometimes comic, but always full of hope."

—MARY GUTERSON, AUTHOR OF *WE ARE ALL FINE HERE*

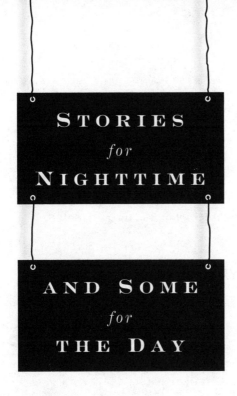

STORIES *for* NIGHTTIME

AND SOME *for* THE DAY

BEN LOORY

PENGUIN BOOKS

PENGUIN BOOKS
Published by the Penguin Group
Penguin Group (USA) Inc., 375 Hudson Street, New York, New York 10014, U.S.A.;
Penguin Group (Canada), 90 Eglinton Avenue East, Suite 700, Toronto, Ontario,
Canada M4P 2Y3 (a division of Pearson Penguin Canada Inc.); Penguin Books Ltd,
80 Strand, London WC2R 0RL, England; Penguin Ireland, 25 St Stephen's Green,
Dublin 2, Ireland (a division of Penguin Books Ltd); Penguin Group (Australia),
250 Camberwell Road, Camberwell, Victoria 3124, Australia (a division of Pearson
Australia Group Pty Ltd); Penguin Books India Pvt Ltd, 11 Community Centre,
Panchsheel Park, New Delhi—110 017, India; Penguin Group (NZ), 67 Apollo Drive,
Rosedale, Auckland 0632, New Zealand (a division of Pearson New Zealand Ltd);
Penguin Books (South Africa) (Pty) Ltd, 24 Sturdee Avenue, Rosebank,
Johannesburg 2196, South Africa

Penguin Books Ltd, Registered Offices:
80 Strand, London WC2R 0RL, England

First published in Penguin Books 2011

10

The following stories were previously published, some in online publications:

"The Book" and "Hadley" in *The Bicycle Review;* "The Swimming Pool" in *Gargoyle
Magazine;* "The Crown" in *Barrelhouse;* "The Man Who Went to China" in *The Antioch
Review;* "The Octopus" in *Girls with Insurance;* "The Path" in *MicroHorror;* "The Hunter's
Head" in *Space and Time;* "The Well" in *JMWW;* "The Shadow" in *escarp;* "Death and the
Fruits of the Tree" in *Leaf Garden;* "The Hat" in *The Collagist;* "The Magic Pig" in *Dogzplot;*
"The Shield" in *Twelve Stories;* "The Little Girl and the Balloon" in *Niteblade;* "The Poet"
in *Writers Bloc;* "The Rope and the Sea" in *Wigleaf;* "The Knife Act" in *Emprise Review;*
"The Fish in the Teapot" in *Bartleby Snopes;* "The Girl in the Storm" in *Apparatus
Magazine;* "The Afterlife Is What You Leave Behind" and "On the Way Down: A Story for
Ray Bradbury" in *Moon Milk Review;* "The Sea Monster" in *Annalemma;* "The End of It
All" in *Necessary Fiction;* "The House on the Cliff and the Sea" in *Thunderclap;* "The Snake
in the Throat" in *A cappella Zoo;* "The Graveyard" in *Flashes in the Dark;* "The Ferris
Wheel" in *Tuesday: An Arts Project;* "The Woman in the Basement" in *PANK;*
and "The TV" in *The New Yorker.*

Publisher's Note
These selections are works of fiction. Names, characters, places, and incidents either are
the product of the author's imagination or are used fictitiously, and any resemblance to
actual persons, living or dead, business establishments, events, or locales
is entirely coincidental.

LIBRARY OF CONGRESS CATALOGING-IN-PUBLICATION DATA
Loory, Ben.
Stories for nighttime and some for the day / Ben Loory.
p. cm.
ISBN 978-0-14-311950-0
I. Title.
PS3612.O57S76 2011
813'.6—dc22
2011012131

Printed in the United States of America
Set in ITC New Baskerville • Designed by Sabrina Bowers

For

Dennis Etchison,

Maureen de Sousa,

my parents, Mel and Barbara Loory,

Andra Moldav,

Sarah Funke Butler,

and

Aline Xavier Mineiro Alvares

Sleep lingers all our lifetime about our eyes,
as night hovers all day in the boughs of the fir-tree.

—EMERSON

A halo is not a helmet.

—JASON VINCZ

CONTENTS

II

III

APPENDIX

AUTHOR'S NOTE

Here are some stories. I hope you like them.

—B.L.

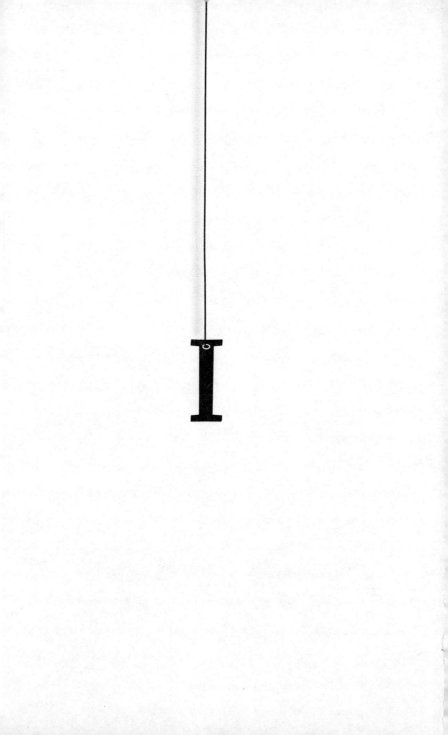

THE BOOK

THE WOMAN RETURNS FROM THE STORE WITH AN armload of books. She reads them quickly, one by one, over the course of the next few weeks. But when she opens the last one, the woman frowns in surprise.

All the pages in the book are blank.

Every single one.

The woman takes the book back to the store, but the manager won't let her return it.

Right there on the cover, the manager says, *This book has no words and is non-returnable.*

The woman is angry. She wouldn't have bought the book if she'd known there were no words inside. But the manager simply will not relent.

The woman leaves in a huff.

She throws the book in the trash.

A few days later, the woman sees a man reading the book on the subway. She gets mad; she screams across the crowded car—

There are no words inside, you can't read it! she says.

But the man becomes defensive.

You can pretend, he says. There's no law against pretending.

I think there might be words if you look at it under a special light, says a woman sitting nearby.

This other woman is holding her own copy of the book.

That's so stupid! the woman yells. Don't you see how stupid that is? Don't you understand that's *crazy*?

At the next station, a policeman is called and has to break up the fight.

A television crew arrives on the scene.

The woman is interviewed. She appears on the news.

She complains loudly about the book for some time.

The next day, the book appears on the bestseller lists, under both fiction and nonfiction. The woman is furious, enraged, appalled. She calls into a radio show and starts to rant. She calls the next day, and the day after that, and then the day after that. She appears again on television, this time in debate with the author.

Your book is a joke! the woman says.

The author just sits there and smiles.

The woman becomes famous for opposing the book. She even writes a book of her own. Her book cries out for the destruction of the first book.

In answer, the first book's sales jump.

The woman is frantic. She doesn't know what to do. She feels like she's going insane.

And then one day on the street a man comes up and spits in the woman's face.

The woman stands there—shocked, paralyzed. She hadn't realized everyone hated her. She turns and runs sobbing all the way home. She locks the door and collapses on the floor.

She crawls into the bedroom on her hands and knees and hides underneath the blankets.

She huddles in the darkness all night long, her hands over her eyes, crying.

The following morning, the woman unplugs her phone. She doesn't want to be invited on TV anymore. She sits on the edge of the bed for a while, and then, slowly, she rises.

The woman turns over a whole new leaf.

She turns her attention to other things.

She takes up hobbies. She goes scuba diving.

She even makes some friends.

Without the controversy the woman's anger stirred up, the book starts to slip from the bestseller lists. It slips and slips for weeks and weeks, until one day it finally disappears.

The woman's own book disappears as well.

The woman doesn't even notice.

The years go by. The woman meets a man. She falls in love and gets married. She has children and raises them and lets them go and watches them start families of their own.

She and her husband go through some hard times, but in the end they stay together.

And then one day, late in life, the woman's husband dies.

For months, the woman is unable to sleep. She wanders through the house, feeling lost. She turns on lights and turns them off. She sits down, gets up, sits.

One evening in the attic, going through her husband's things, the woman finds a copy of the book.

She hasn't thought of the book in years.

She's afraid to open it up.

Instead, she takes the book back downstairs and puts it on the shelf. It sits there untouched for weeks and weeks, until one day her grandchildren come over.

What's this? one of them says, and lifts it up, and as she does something falls out.

The woman reaches down and picks it up.

It's a single old photograph.

It's a picture taken of her and her husband on the very first day they met. They're standing together on the beach; in the distance is a sunset.

Oh, says the woman, look at that.

And a smile spreads across her face.

And then the book seems to open itself, and there's her life on the page.

THE SWIMMING POOL

THE MAN STOPS BY THE PUBLIC POOL ON HIS WAY HOME from work. It's something he does from time to time. He enjoys the laughter, the splashing, the sound of feet slapping concrete. He stands by the fence, taking it all in.

That's when he sees the shark.

Shark! the man yells, waving his arms. Shark! Shark! Shark!

Everyone turns and looks at him—children, parents, the lifeguard.

That's not very funny, says a woman nearby.

It's not supposed to be funny! yells the man. There's a shark in the pool! See it—right there!

But even then, he's no longer sure. How could there be a shark in a public pool? It doesn't make any sense. And now he can no longer see any sign of it.

He watches awhile longer, then turns to head home. Everyone stares after him as he goes.

That night the man cannot sleep. He keeps seeing the shark in his mind. Eventually he gets up and puts on his clothes. He walks back down to the pool.

The overhead lights are out when he gets there, and he finds that the gates are locked. He climbs the fence—with a great deal of effort—and drops down to the other side.

He pads silently around the water's edge, staring down into the dark. A couple of times he thinks he sees something, but each time it's just a ripple, a trick of the light.

In the morning, the man goes by the pool on the way to work. The lifeguard is out, skimming leaves. Otherwise the pool is quiet, deserted.

The man stops at the fence.

You ever see anything in there? he asks the lifeguard.

The lifeguard turns and looks at him.

What do you mean, *anything*? he says suspiciously.

I don't know, the man says. Fish?

The lifeguard tilts his head.

You the guy from yesterday? he says.

The man hesitates.

Yes, he says.

The lifeguard considers. He takes a step forward.

It's an odd thing, he says, glancing around, but sometimes I *do* seem to see things. Things that shouldn't be there.

Like what? says the man. Things like what?

I don't know, shrugs the lifeguard. Just things.

Anyway, he says, suddenly snapping out of it, you don't have to worry, it's not your job.

And the lifeguard turns and goes back to work.

And the man continues on.

But all day long the man thinks to himself: What kind of things did the lifeguard see? And what did he mean, it's not my job? As though anyone could ignore a shark in a public pool.

The man goes to the pool again that night. This time he climbs up on the diving board. He stretches out at the end, facedown on his belly, and stares into the darkness of the deep end.

He stares down for hours, for hours and hours, searching, searching, seeing nothing.

And then, finally, just before dawn, he sees it.

The man sees the monster.

It is a tremendous thing, the monster below—so big the man missed it before. It is jet-black and featureless and lying stretched out, covering the entire bottom of the pool.

And the worst thing is that it is staring at the man—staring right back up at him. Staring at him with black, unblinking eyes.

It must have been staring the whole time.

The man is seized by a terrible fear. If it should jump, he thinks, if it should leap for him! He'd be lost—lost completely—he'd be taken, he'd die.

Slowly, he backs off the diving board.

He climbs down to the pavement, then scrambles up the fence and jumps over and runs for his house. Overhead, the streetlights flicker and dim. The man closes his eyes and runs.

He prays the trees will all just be trees, and the wind will just be the wind. He prays the ground will just be the ground.

He prays just to make it home.

Once in his house, the man turns on all the lights. Then he goes and sits in the kitchen. He sits at the table with the radio blaring until the sun finally rises in the morning.

Only then does the man's terror subside.

Or, if not subside, at least lessen.

But the thing in the pool! What about the children? What about the children of the neighborhood? Every day they swim in there! They take their lives in their hands! And none of them—or their parents—even know!

The man begins a campaign to have the pool closed. He scours old newspapers at the library. He finds a few articles detailing accidents, near drownings—even a number of deaths.

There are town council meetings, lawyers, a courtroom; eventually the man wins the suit. The public pool is declared officially unsafe, and a date is set for its closure.

The day they finally drain the water from the pool, the man stands in attendance. And as the water level sinks lower and lower, his breath comes more easily to him.

But when the pool lies dry and bare, like a great white empty shell, the man does not feel the triumph he'd expected. Instead, he feels empty, alone.

What's wrong? the man says, as he falls to his knees.

What's wrong? he whispers. Please, tell me.

And then, with the night, the answer comes.

He's set the monster free.

THE TUNNEL

TWO BOYS ARE WALKING HOME FROM SCHOOL WHEN ONE of them sees a drainpipe set back in the woods.

Look at that, the boy says. I never knew that was there. Let's go in and see where it goes.

But the other boy takes one look at the pipe and quickly shakes his head.

Uh-uh, he says. Not me. No way.

Why not? says the first boy. Are you scared?

I just don't want to, his friend says, and takes a single step back.

Come on, says the first boy. It's just a pipe.

But the other boy won't be swayed.

I'll see you later, he says.

And then he turns around and runs.

The first boy watches as his friend disappears, and then he turns again to the pipe. Its open mouth is very dark, and very, very wide.

The boy glances around as he moves towards it.
He is all alone.

When he gets to the opening, the boy peers inside,
but he can't see anything in the dark. Scraggly vines
spill over the edge and hang down to the leaf-strewn
ground.

The boy leans forward and yells into the pipe. He
waits for the echo to come back.

But nothing ever comes back, no sound at all—just
silence—although he waits and waits.

The boy climbs up onto the lip of the pipe and kneels,
facing into the dark.

All right, he thinks. Here we go. Just keep crawling
until you reach the end.

The going is very slow at first. The boy has to be careful.
The floor of the pipe is littered with rocks that gouge his
hands and knees.

But after some time, the debris seems to clear, and
then the crawling gets easier.

The boy crawls until the daylight diminishes to a pin-
point behind him and disappears.

Now enveloped by the dark, the boy waits for his eyes to
adjust. But this never happens, not even in the least, no
matter how long he waits.

Finally, he decides to give it up, and crawls onward, blind. He feels his way through the pipe with wary, outstretched hands.

I'm just in a pipe, he keeps telling himself. I'm just in a pipe, that's all. There's no reason to be afraid. Eventually I'll get to the end.

But the thing is—the boy finds—the tunnel has no end. Or, at least, none he ever reaches. Instead, the tunnel closes in—bit by bit, slowly. It grows smaller, gradually; narrower, narrower, tighter. The boy can feel the roof pressing down, the sides squeezing in. His ribs contract; air hisses from his lungs. But still he fights to move on, to press ahead, to push through.

Until—suddenly—he realizes he couldn't turn around if he tried.

The boy's flat on the ground now, with the ceiling on his back. Filthy walls press his arms against his sides. He pants as he inches forward through some foul-smelling substance. He can hardly breathe; his head is starting to spin.

And then the boy feels it—he feels the tunnel grab him. From all around, it takes him, holds him fast.

The boy screams and squirms—but he's trapped, immobilized. It's no use; he can't move at all.

And as he lies there in the dark, a single thought comes to him.

The single thought fills his mind.

He is going to die.

And it is then—and only then—that the boy sees the door. The little door in the wall right before him.

He reaches out and touches it, runs a hand over its surface. It's real, all right—not a dream.

He slowly turns the knob.

The door creaks open to reveal a quiet, peaceful room. Moonlight spills in through the window. There's a bed—a small bed—with a figure lying in it.

The figure stirs and looks up.

It's the boy's friend who ran away.

The boy watches as his friend in the bed shrinks back against the wall, and then he takes a step down from the pipe.

He moves slowly, deliberately, trailing leaves and rocks and oily tracks, and a crooked smile cracks his face.

Please don't scream, he says.

But his friend in the bed doesn't obey. His mouth opens wide and he screams.

So the boy reaches out with one gnarled, twisted claw.

Together the two boys reach the end.

THE CROWN

A MAN WORKS AS A DISHWASHER.

One day, as he is rinsing the dishes, he finds something strange in the water. He takes it out and looks at it, but it appears to be invisible.

He collars a passing busboy.

Hey, what is this? he says.

The busboy takes it and feels it with his hands.

It's a crown, he says, and gives a shrug.

Then he hands it back and walks away.

The man looks down at the invisible thing in his hands.

A crown? he thinks. In my dishwater?

It doesn't make sense. The man shakes his head, then sets the crown on the drying rack and goes back to work.

Later, when his shift is over, he forgets all about it and goes home.

But the next day, the crown is in his dishwater again.

This again! thinks the man. Why is this here?

At first he's angry, but then he gets an idea. He dries off the crown and puts it on his head.

He spends some time getting used to the feeling.

It's kinda nice to wear a crown, he decides.

It seems to make him work just a little bit harder.

He even starts to whistle a little tune.

The days go by, and the man gets used to the crown. He's never felt so good about himself. He actually starts to find himself looking forward to going to work.

This is a new experience for him.

The only thing the man finds just a little sad is that no one but him is aware of his crown.

My crown is so nice, the man keeps thinking. I wish it wasn't quite so invisible.

Then one night at home, while watching TV, the man suddenly has a great idea. He takes off his crown and looks at it—or tries to—and then he goes out into the garage. He hunts all around until he finds the paint cans, and then he sits down on the floor with a brush. He paints the crown a bright, bright yellow—the brightest yellow he has. It takes him a little time to paint it evenly, but it comes out nicely in the end.

The man sits there and looks at the crown in his hands. It is strange to see it so yellow. Actually, it is strange to see it at all. But in any case, the man finds it delightful.

He can't wait to show it off at work.

But the thing is, the next day, the man never gets to work. He is surrounded as he walks down the street.

The king! The king! everyone is saying. Look, everybody, it's the king!

The man smiles and tries to act appropriately, but the people are swarming around him. They are yelling and yelling. He can hardly move. Everyone is talking to him.

Oh, king, they are saying, please help us! We need money, and food, and housing! And more days off, and a nicer flag, and teachers and schools and tanks! We need a man to walk on the moon again! We need a better system of transit! We need bigger farms and a cure for cancer! No, scratch that—a cure for death!

The man doesn't know what to say to anyone. Mostly he just kind of nods. Pretty soon he's in a long limousine with men wearing fancy suits. Everyone is talking very excitedly about things the man doesn't understand. He keeps having to sign official-looking documents and pose for pictures and shake people's hands.

Eventually the man is sitting on a throne in an immense room with tapestries on the walls, and rows of buglers are serenading him with big, loud, shiny horns.

It comes down to this: there is another country—some country somewhere—and they are about to attack.

The men who swarm about the king's throne swear up and down to this fact. These other countries—did I say it was just one?—are going to strike at any moment, and what is the king going to do about it? Will he, or will he not, unleash the bombs?

The king excuses himself and goes into the bathroom. He stands there, staring into the mirror.

How did I get to be king? he thinks. All I wanted was a raise.

The man takes off his crown and looks at it. It is quite silly, actually, he now sees—the yellow paint is garishly bright, and much of it is flaking away. He reaches out and slowly turns on the tap, then holds the crown underneath, and quietly washes the paint away, scrubbing frantically with a paper towel to help speed up the process.

Finally, when the crown is no longer visible, the man turns to throw it in the trash. But then he stops, having suddenly noticed that there is nothing in his hand.

Visible or invisible—there's nothing there.

The man turns and looks back at the sink.

The sink too, he sees, is completely empty.

The crown must have melted away.

Outside, in the hall, the king's retainers are waiting.

I'm sorry, the man says, with empty hands. I seem to

have lost my crown, as you see. I'd like to help, but it looks like I can't be king.

And in answer, the buglers all blow their bugles, and every man present—as one—reaches behind his back and holds out to the man a gleaming crown of solid gold.

THE MAN WHO WENT TO CHINA

ONCE UPON A TIME, A MAN WENT TO CHINA. THEN, later on, he came back. This was at a time when people didn't go to China—it was a strange place, and far away, like something in a book. But this man went, and then later, he came back. And when he came back, he was rich.

He'd traded things for other things, the usual things, expensive things; there really isn't much to speak of there.

The only matter of interest to us is the box—the small lacquered box he came back holding in his hand.

It was in his hand all the time, either one hand or the other—though sometimes, when seated, he'd rest it on his lap. But even then, he was always touching it, caressing it, smoothing it, as if making sure that it was there, or assuring it that he was.

The man was not (of course) Chinese, but he dressed and acted as though he were. And for this reason, those in the town who knew of him referred to him as the Chinaman.

He lived in a large, Oriental-looking house on a hill overlooking the town. Every morning he sat and took tea on his porch, and every morning the box sat with him.

The neighborhood boys soon took notice, and they began to argue about what was in the box.

It is a treasure, one said. The Chinaman's greatest treasure—a magical amulet that lengthens a man's life.

No, said another, it is a photograph of his wife—the Chinese wife he left behind.

No, said a third, I think you're both wrong. It is his last will and testament.

And the guesses went on until the boys finally realized there was only one way to know the truth. One of them would have to go and sneak into the house, and find and open up the little box.

Only one boy volunteered.

He was a small boy, and poor. He had never done much, and always clamored for more.

He looked around and saw that only his hand was up.

At first, he was frightened.

But then he grew resolved.

That night the boy crept into the Chinaman's house. He wound his way through the maze of artifacts. He went under the birdcages and over the carpets, and around the tall painted screens.

As he approached the Chinaman's bedroom, the boy's heart began to pound. He stood in the doorway for a while. He stared into the darkness, waiting for his eyes to adjust. And then they did, and he saw.

There was the Chinaman, asleep in his bed, underneath his fine silk sheets.

And there, on the pillow resting beside him—unheld—was the small, lacquered box.

The boy moved closer. He moved very quietly. He reached toward the box with one hand.

The Chinaman issued a small, sad sigh as the boy lifted the box, but slept on.

In the adjoining room, the boy sat on the floor and started to open the box. His personal belief was that it would hold sweets, and his stomach was aching with hunger.

He turned a small latch, and a drawer slid open.

Inside the drawer was a tiny man.

The man was smaller than the boy's little finger, and bound hand and foot with threadlike ropes. A tiny black bag covered his head and was tied tightly about his throat.

Despite that, however, the man was alive.

The front of the bag rose and fell.

With trembling fingers, the boy started to undo the knot that held the bag closed. And when he was done, he loosened the string and gently lifted off the hood.

There was the Chinaman, staring back up at him. A minuscule version of the man. With a gag in his mouth, his eyes wide with panic—lost—completely lost. Terrified.

The boy's mind reeled as he stared at the tiny Chinaman. This one looked younger than the real one. His hair was shorter, his skin was smoother; he had an entirely different air about him.

Less Oriental, one might say. Less traveled, less knowing, less wise.

Please, said a voice then, put him back in the box.

The real Chinaman stood in the doorway.

This is yours, he said, jingling a small leather pouch, if you put him back as he was.

The boy looked down at the man in the box.

But what is he? he wanted to know.

He is nothing, said the Chinaman. Just as he always was. Now be fast, or all will be lost.

The Chinaman tossed the bag of gold to the floor, and it spilled open before the boy's feet. The boy looked from the clattering coins to the face of the frightened, imprisoned little man.

Do you feed him? said the boy. What does he eat?

He doesn't, said the Chinaman. Now come. There is a fortune there waiting. Put back the hood, close the drawer, and pick up the gold.

And so the boy lowered the bag into place, and slid the drawer back into the box.

Wait here, said the Chinaman, taking it from him. Wait, and I will be back.

He was gone for some time, while the boy gathered his gold. The Chinaman returned with a box of kitchen matches.

Take this, he said, handing it to the boy.

The boy opened it, looked inside, and frowned.

It's empty, he said, shaking it to be sure.

Yes, said the Chinaman. But things change.

The next day, the neighborhood boys sat and waited for the boy to come and tell them what was in the box. But the boy never came, though they waited all day, and finally they grew concerned. They went to the house where they knew he sometimes stayed and found he'd never come home the night before. They searched the whole town, but no one had seen him.

They looked up to the house on the hill.

They approached it slowly, and stood outside. It was calm, and very quiet. They knocked on the door, and the door swung open.

The house was empty; the Chinaman was gone.

And not just the Chinaman—all of his things. All his furniture, his paintings, his screens.

The only thing they found was the small, lacquered box, which they opened, but it didn't contain a thing.

THE OCTOPUS

THE OCTOPUS IS SPOONING SUGAR INTO HIS TEA WHEN there is a knock on the door.

Come in, says the octopus over his shoulder, and the door opens.

It is Mrs. Jorgenson.

Got your mail, Mr. Octopus, she says, moving daintily into the apartment.

Thank you, Mrs. Jorgenson, says the octopus. Would you like some tea?

Why yes, I'd love some, comes the response. Do you mind if I sit down?

Not at all, says the octopus, getting down another cup. Not at all.

He brings the tea to the table.

Oh, my aching feet, says Mrs. Jorgenson. I've been up and down those stairs so many times today already.

I do appreciate your bringing up my mail, says the octopus, laying a spoon beside the sugar bowl for Mrs. Jorgenson.

Oh, for you I don't mind at all, she says. It's just some

of these other tenants. Everyone's got a problem, you know. And I nearly tripped and fell on the third floor; there was some kind of puddle.

Puddle? says the octopus.

Puddle! says Mrs. Jorgenson. Just sitting there in the middle of the staircase.

The octopus looks confused. Then he sees the mail.

Do you mind if I . . . ? he says to Mrs. Jorgenson.

Heavens, no, she replies. You go right ahead. Mmm, this is good tea.

Darjeeling, says the octopus, leafing through the mail.

There's really nothing good, just the usual stuff. Bills, catalogs, junk mail, more bills . . . and then the octopus gets to the last piece of mail. He sits there, holding it gently in one tentacle.

What is it? says Mrs. Jorgenson.

It's from the ocean, says the octopus, staring at the postmark.

I didn't know you still had folks there, says Mrs. Jorgenson.

Oh yes, says the octopus. Oh yes, I do. My brother, my brother's children.

How nice, says Mrs. Jorgenson. Perhaps it's from them?

Perhaps it is, says the octopus, and slits the envelope open.

He reads for some time.

Hmm, he says, when he gets to the end.

He looks up to see Mrs. Jorgenson staring at him.

It's from my little nephews, he says. Would you like me to read it?

I wouldn't dream of it, says Mrs. Jorgenson. I mean, unless you wanted to.

The octopus smiles and holds up the letter again. He begins to read.

Dear Uncle Harley, he reads—interjecting, *My name is Harley*—Hello from the ocean! We hope everything on land is going well. The other day Aunt Hattie got into a fight with a cuttlefish. It was funny! We think we might like to come visit you, just the two of us. We've heard so much about you, we'd like to meet you in person. Would that be okay? Please let us know. Your nephews, Gerald and Lewis.

He finishes reading and lowers the letter.

Gerald and Lewis, says Mrs. Jorgenson. They sound like nice young boys.

Oh, they are, says the octopus. Or at least, so it seems. I never really met them in person. I mean, they were only just hatched when I left, so they hadn't quite developed personalities.

Ah, says Mrs. Jorgenson. Are you going to let them come?

Well, says the octopus, looking around, I don't really have a lot of room. Just the couch, really. Where would the other one sleep?

I have a cot I could bring up, says Mrs. Jorgenson.

Do you? says the octopus. Well, that would work. It would be nice to see some of the old gang again.

How long have you been here? asks Mrs. Jorgenson.

About fifteen years, says the octopus.

That's a long time, says Mrs. Jorgenson.

Yes, but I love it, says the octopus, looking around at his apartment. Yes, but I do love it so.

Well, says Mrs. Jorgenson, I guess you should be writing back. If you dash something off, I'll put it in the mailbox when I get down to the lobby.

Would you? says the octopus.

Yes, of course, says Mrs. Jorgenson.

And so it is done.

A few days later there is a knock on the door.

Come in, hollers the octopus, who is cleaning his spoons.

But the door does not open. The octopus grumbles a bit, then gets down from his chair and glides across the room. He opens the door a crack.

Gerald and Lewis! he says, in surprise.

Uncle Harley! they say, and they all embrace.

Come in, come in, says the octopus.

Gerald and Lewis move inside the apartment.

So this is what an apartment looks like, says Gerald, his eyes roving over everything.

It's a little dirty right now, says the octopus.

Dirty? says Gerald. It's amazing—so many treasures!

He is looking at the octopus's collection of spoons, laid out on the table for polishing.

Those are my spoons, says the octopus. I collect them.

What are they for? says Lewis. His voice is rather squeaky.

They're for moving small volumes of liquid around,

says the octopus. Or solids, like sugar. I use them all the time.

All three octopi stand there and stare at the spoons.

We don't have anything like that in the ocean, says Gerald.

No, says the octopus, you don't.

Well, he says suddenly, turning. Gerald, you will have the couch. And Lewis, you will have the cot. Unless you want to trade off from night to night.

No, that will be fine, says Lewis. I don't mind. I've never slept on a cot before.

He goes and sits on the cot. He bounces up and down.

So where will we go first? he asks.

Go? says the octopus, looking at him.

Go, says Lewis. What will we go to see first?

The octopus doesn't know what to say.

You mean in the, in the city? he asks.

Of course, says Lewis. We just came from the ocean.

Oh, well, I don't know, says the octopus. I don't really go out there.

You don't go into the city? says Lewis.

No, says the octopus. Not really.

Ever? says Lewis.

No, says the octopus. I like it here.

Gerald and Lewis look at each other.

We thought you were going to take us around to see the city, Gerald says. That's why we came.

I thought you came to see me, says the octopus.

Well, that too, of course, says Gerald. It was both, it was both.

They said we could only come if you'd show us around and take care of us, says Lewis.

Who? says the octopus. Who said that?

Daddy and Aunt Hattie, says Lewis.

Ah, says the octopus. I see.

And now we're here, says Lewis.

Indeed, you are, says the octopus.

The three octopi regard one another in silence.

Well, I guess I'll be being your tour guide, the octopus says, finally.

Gerald and Lewis smile broadly.

They spend the next day walking the streets of the city. Gerald has a map, and Lewis is in charge of sunscreen. The octopus himself merely walks, staring up at the huge, awe-inspiring buildings and trying not to be terrified of the passing buses and cars.

You're more scared than we are, Uncle Harley, says Gerald.

And Lewis and the octopus both laugh.

They go to the museums and libraries. They listen to a concert in a park. They have lunch and dinner, and go to an opera.

At the end of the day, they find themselves sitting at an outdoor café. Gerald and Lewis are drinking root beer; the octopus has tea.

So? says the octopus. What do you think?

It certainly is large, says Gerald.

It certainly is huge, says Lewis.

The octopus nods.

Yes it is, he says. Yes, it is.

It is true that you'll live forever? says Gerald out of the blue. I mean, if you stay here?

The octopus looks at him thoughtfully.

It is, says the octopus. It is true. Supposedly, of course. I guess the only way to tell for sure is to stay here and find out.

But why does it work that way? says Lewis. Why can't we live forever in the ocean?

I don't know, says the octopus. That's just the way it is. When an octopus comes to land, he lives forever. It's just the way it is, like the way some people have brown hair and some people are blond.

Gerald and Lewis sit and stare at their sodas.

Has Dad ever been here? Gerald asks.

No, says the octopus. Your dad was never much interested in land.

Why's that? says Lewis.

I don't know, says the octopus. He just wasn't. He met your mom and they were very happy, and then they had you. So there was never really time for coming to visit the land, or for thinking about living here.

But why don't we all live here? says Gerald.

The octopus looks at him and smiles.

It just doesn't work that way, he says. It just doesn't work that way.

That night the octopus tucks Gerald and Lewis into bed.

Sleep tight, he says. Tomorrow you go back to the ocean.

What? Already? say Gerald and Lewis.

I'm sorry, says the octopus, but yes. I have a lot of things to do and I can't do them with you boys hanging around all the time. I love you, though. You boys know that?

The boys grumble a little, but say yes.

Good, says the octopus. Then good night.

He pats the boys on their heads and then goes into the kitchen. He makes himself a cup of tea and stirs sugar into it with a spoon. He listens to the clanking noise the spoon makes against the cup, and watches the liquid as it swirls around: a circle, a circle, a circle, circle.

When he returns to the living room, the boys are fast asleep. He stands there in the darkness, watching them. Then he returns to the kitchen and opens a cabinet. Inside, the silver polish; in the drawer, the spoons.

The next morning they are all off to the beach.

Shall I carry your suitcase? the octopus says to Lewis.

Oh no, says Lewis, I got it.

They move down the staircase. In the lobby, they pass Mrs. Jorgenson.

Why Mr. Octopus, says Mrs. Jorgenson, you're out and about!

Just taking the boys back to the sea, says the octopus, and the boys wave hello and good-bye.

They take the subway to the beach. The subway is very crowded.

Where are all these people going? says Gerald. There are so many of them.

I don't know, says the octopus, looking around. I always wondered that myself.

When they get to the beach, Gerald and Lewis trudge down to the waterline.

Are you sure we can't stay with you another day? asks Gerald.

I'm positive, says the octopus. I'm sorry.

But why can't we stay? says Lewis.

There's no reason, says the octopus. I just can't let you. Please, boys, just do as you're told.

The boys grumble some more, but they're not really angry. They give the octopus great big hugs.

Good-bye, Uncle Harley, Gerald says.

Good-bye, Uncle, says Lewis.

Good-bye, boys, says the octopus. Now off with you.

And he stands there and watches as the boys slap down into the surf and wade out beneath the waves.

Thank God that's over, thinks the octopus. Now I can go back to my life.

But, strangely, the octopus does not turn. Instead, he stands there and stares—off into the gently rolling surf, down into the water, after Gerald and Lewis. In his mind the octopus pictures his brother—their father—and poor Aunt Hattie, and all those other octopi he used to know in the days before he lived on land. He remembers the day he turned away from them—the day he swam away—the day he walked up onto the beach, and headed into the city and found the apartment. He remembers the day he began drinking tea, and the day he started collecting spoons. He remembers the day he stopped getting his mail and let Mrs. Jorgenson bring it up to him. He remembers in turn all of these things, all of them and more. He remembers the tea as it swirled around and around in a circle in his cup.

The octopus suddenly finds himself walking down the beach to the water. He feels the sand under his tentacles, and then the water washing over them.

My god, the water feels good, he thinks. I had almost forgotten.

He stands in the shallows, gazing out, and then, in one motion, he dives in.

The octopus swims toward the depths—his tentacles waving free—and something inside him opens up. Suddenly, he can breathe.

I'm coming, brother, he calls out, in his mind and in the sea. I'm coming, nephews. I'm coming, friends. I'm coming home. It's me!

THE PATH

THE MAN IS ON A PATH. IT IS A FUNNY THING. LIFE SORT of gives him hints. Just before the phone rings, the man will look over. When he gets an urge to play the lottery, he wins.

The man has a job and he does it very well. Everything comes easily to him. He makes the right calls; he says the right things; he gets raises and benefits and perks.

Then one day the man is walking home from work, when suddenly he is hit by a car.

The man wakes up in the hospital. He doesn't understand.

Me? he says. Hit by a car?

He looks around. It doesn't make sense.

And that's when he sees—his path is gone.

The path he's always been on is gone.

The man doesn't know what to do anymore. *How* to— how to do *anything*. He doesn't even know how to work the water fountain, can't figure out when it's time to go to the bathroom.

His wife and children come to visit; the man doesn't know their names.

Is there something wrong with his brain? his wife says.

The doctor shakes his head.

He's just thrown a little, he says to the wife. From the accident, you know. He'll be fine.

But the man isn't fine—that's the thing. When he's discharged, he goes back to work. But he's just no good at his job anymore; he has no idea how to do it. He can't even find the office half the time—and when he does somehow manage to stumble in, he sits behind his desk staring out at the clouds as they drift back and forth across the sky.

The man's wife is worried—she doesn't understand—so the man finally tells her about the path.

It used to be there, he explains, and now it's gone.

His wife doesn't know what to say.

She puts her arms around him, and holds him close, and leads him down the hallway to bed.

But like all the other things that used to come so easily, this one doesn't come anymore.

The man begins to take long walks late at night. He wanders around in circles, aimlessly. Then one morning he comes home to find that his wife and his children are gone.

The man stands in the bathroom with the gun to his head. Slowly, he pulls the trigger. He hears the shot—and then five more.

He lowers the gun and looks over.

There are six holes in the wall, right beside his head. Six little round, perfect holes.

But there are no holes at all in the man's head.

There are no holes there at all.

The man finds himself walking from the bathroom. He finds himself leaving the house. He finds himself walking across the street, through a bus, a park bench, an empty lot.

The man finds himself walking and walking, walking on and on. The path that he walks on is always a straight line, and the straight line always leads him on.

The man never thinks about where he's going; he never thinks about turning back. As for his life—his children and his wife—the man put a line through all that.

He walks off.

THE HUNTER'S HEAD

A HUNTER RETURNS TO HIS VILLAGE ONE NIGHT WITH A severed human head in one hand. He jams the head onto a stake and sticks it into the ground by his hut.

Then he goes inside and falls asleep.

The people of the village stand at a distance and stare at the head in horror. They mutter among themselves all night long and worry about what the hunter has done.

But in the morning, when the hunter emerges from his hut and heads back out into the jungle, none of them says a single word; they just stand and watch him as he goes.

Then, when he's gone, they turn as one to look at the head again. But none of them has the courage to approach it.

Except for one small boy.

The severed head, it turns out, is that of a woman. A young woman, neither beautiful nor ugly.

The boy stares at it in silence for a moment.

Then the head opens its eyes.

Boo! it says, and the boy jumps.

Sorry, says the head, didn't mean to scare you.

I thought you were dead, the boy says.

Dead? says the head. What do you mean?

The boy doesn't know how to answer.

The head's eyes wander around.

Where am I? it says. This doesn't look familiar.

You're in our village, says the boy.

Did *you* come from a village? he adds a moment later.

A village? says the head. I don't remember.

It frowns for a while as it seems to think.

I can't remember very much, it says.

The head seems sad, so the boy tries to cheer it up. He tells the head stories about his life. He tells it the story about the time his brother got his toe bitten off by a raccoon.

The head laughs and laughs and laughs and laughs.

Then the hunter returns from the jungle.

This time he is carrying two heads.

He doesn't seem to notice the boy as he affixes the heads to stakes. He jams the stakes down into the ground just like he did the first.

Where are these heads coming from? says the boy.

But the hunter walks right past him, goes inside the hut, and falls asleep.

The boy looks over at the two new heads. They open their eyes and stare back at him.

Who are you? the two new heads say.

A boy, says the first head. His brother lost a toe to a raccoon.

Ah, the two new heads say.

They look at the boy.

Ah, they say.

In the morning, the boy rises early and follows the hunter into the jungle. The hunter moves quickly; it is hard to keep up, and it gets harder and harder as they go.

The boy follows the hunter all day; he loses all track of where he is. All he knows is he's farther from his village than he's ever been in his life.

But eventually—eventually—the hunter starts to slow.

He stops behind a tree and looks out.

Then he readies his machete and spear.

The boy looks out to follow the hunter's gaze. There is a village in the clearing beyond the tree. And it is full of villagers—just like those back home—going peacefully about their lives. They are talking and laughing and carrying on, just as though nothing were happening. Just as though no one were hiding behind the tree, getting ready to jump out and kill them.

The hunter charges. The villagers panic. They scream and shout, but there's nothing they can do. The hunter chops and stabs and spears and clubs them, and hacks off three more heads. Then he gathers the heads up into his arms and runs back into the jungle again.

He runs—unseeing—right past the boy.

A moment later, the villagers come after him.

The boy takes off running after the hunter, with the villagers behind in pursuit. The boy runs for his life, without looking back; he runs as fast as he can. He runs until his heart thumps in his chest and all he can hear is his breath. And, in his mind, he hears the screams of villagers as the hunter hacked them to death.

Somehow, the boy makes it back to his own village alive, with his pursuers left behind.

And there he finds the hunter already by his hut, jamming the three new heads into the ground.

Late that night the boy enters the hunter's hut and stands over him in the dark. He wants to know why the hunter kills those people, wants to know why he chops off their heads. But there is nothing about the hunter's sleeping form that explains anything to the boy—anything at all about what's in his mind, why he does the things that he does.

When the boy finally turns and steps from the hut, he finds six severed heads out there waiting.

You have to kill him, says the first.

You have to do it, says the second.

You're the only one who can, says the third.

If not you, then who? the three others say.

If not you, then who? the heads say.

The next day the boy hides in the shadows of his mother's hut and watches the severed heads as they talk. He can't hear what they're saying, but he knows it's about him—their eyes keep glancing his way.

The boy is holding a knife in his hand—a small knife he found in the dirt.

He feels the edge of the blade with his thumb.

He winces as it threatens to break the skin.

That evening when the hunter returns from the jungle, he doesn't even bother with the stakes. He just dumps all the heads he's carrying in a pile by his hut and goes inside and lies down to sleep.

The boy stares at the pile of heads, and the heads in the pile stare back.

Some time passes.

And then some more.

And then it gets very dark.

The boy rises from his hiding place and steps forward.

Do it, whispers one of the heads. Think of his head as a toe, it says. Be like the raccoon, it says.

Do it for us, says another head. And so there will never be any more.

Do it, say the rest. Do it, do it.

Do it, say all of the heads.

And so the boy does it.

There is a lot of blood, and it takes quite some time. But when he finally emerges from the hut with the head, the boy's mind feels strangely calm.

He places the hunter's head on a stake and jams it into the ground.

The other heads have closed their eyes.

The boy slips into the jungle and is gone.

THE DUCK

A DUCK FELL IN LOVE WITH A ROCK. IT WAS A LARGE rock—about the size of a duck, actually—that was situated off the bank of the river a little past the old elm. Every day after lunch the duck would saunter off to admire the rock for a while.

Where are you going? said the other ducks.

Nowhere, said the duck. Just around.

But the other ducks knew exactly where he was going and they all laughed at him behind his back.

Stupid duck is in love with a rock, they sniggered. Wonder what kind of ducklings they will have.

But there was one duck—a girl duck—who did not laugh. She had known the strange duck for a long time, and had always found him to be a good and decent bird. She felt sorry for him; it was hard luck to fall in love with a rock. She wanted to help, but what could she do? She trailed after the duck and watched him woo the rock from behind a tree.

I love you, the duck was saying. I love you I love you I love you. I love you more than the stars in the sky, I love you more than the fish in the river, I love you more than . . . more than . . .

There he stopped, for he could think of nothing else that existed.

Life itself? said the girl duck from behind the tree. She hadn't meant to pipe up. The words just sort of leapt out of her.

The duck spun around to look at her. He was terrified.

It's okay, said the girl duck, waddling out from behind the tree. I know you're in love with the rock. In fact, everyone knows.

They do? said the duck.

Yes, said the girl duck. Yes, they do.

The duck sighed and sat down on the ground. If he had had hands, he would have buried his head in them.

What am I going to do? he said. What am I going to do?

Do? the girl duck said.

How can it go on like this? said the duck. I love a thing that cannot speak, cannot move, cannot . . . I don't even know how it feels about me!

The girl duck looked at the rock. She didn't know what to say.

I know, said the duck. You think I'm crazy. You think it's just a rock. But it isn't just a rock; it's different. It's very different.

He looked at the rock.

But something has to happen, he said, and soon. Because my heart will break if this goes on much longer.

That night the girl duck had a hard time sleeping. She kept paddling around in circles, thinking about the rock and the duck and his heart that might break. She thought long and hard, and before morning she had an idea. She went and woke up the strange duck.

Things happen when they must, she said, as if it were an extremely meaningful statement.

So? said the duck.

So I have a plan, said the girl duck. And I think that it will work.

Well what is it? said the duck, nearly bursting with excitement.

We will need help, said the girl duck, and it will take some time. And also we will need a cliff.

Two days later they set out. It took four ducks to carry the rock. They worked in teams and traded off every fifteen minutes. Everyone joined in, even though they'd laughed, for ducks are all brothers when it comes right down to it.

The cliff is over that hill and then quite a ways to the south, said the most elderly duck. I remember flying over it when I was a fledgling. It looked like the edge of the world.

The ducks trudged on under their rocky weight for

hours—for hours, and then for days. At night they camped under hedges and strange trees and ate beetles and frogs.

Do you think it will be much farther? said one of the ducks.

Maybe, said the oldest duck. My memory is not so good anymore.

On the sixth day, the ducks began to tire.

I don't believe there is a cliff, said one of them.

Me neither, said another. I think the old duck is crazy.

My back hurts, said a third duck. I want to go home.

Me too, said a fourth. In fact, I'm going to.

And then all the ducks began to turn for home. The rock fell to the forest floor and lay there.

The strange duck looked imploringly at the girl duck.

Don't worry, she said, I won't leave you.

They watched all the other ducks flee homeward, and then they hoisted the rock onto their backs and trudged on.

What do you think will happen when we throw it off the cliff? said the duck.

I don't know, said the girl duck. I just know it will be something.

Finally they came to the edge of the cliff. The drop-off was so great they couldn't see the ground—just great white clouds spread out before them like an endless rolling cotton blanket.

It looks so soft, said the duck.

Yes it does, said the girl duck. Are you ready?

The duck looked at the rock.

This is it, my love, he said. The moment of truth. And whatever happens, please remember—always remember— I love you.

And the two ducks hurled the rock off the cliff together.

At first the rock simply fell. Like a rock, one might say. Like a stone.

But then something began to happen. It began to slow, it began to grow, it began to change. It narrowed, it elongated—and it also spread sideways.

It's becoming a bird, the girl duck said.

And it was. It was becoming a beautiful gray bird— really not that unlike a duck. Its wings began to move slowly up and down, up and down, and it dove down and then coasted up. It looked back over its shoulder at the two ducks on the cliff, and it called out just once—Goodbye! And then it was going, going, getting smaller and smaller, flying off, over the blanket, across the sky.

The ducks did not speak much on the way home.

Do you think it will be happy? said the duck.

I hope so, said the girl duck, and that was all.

They really didn't say any more.

When they reached the pond, the other ducks gathered around and clamored to hear what had happened. The duck and the girl duck glanced at each other.

Nothing, said the girl duck. It fell.

In the days that followed, the duck stayed to himself. The girl duck went and swam around in circles. She thought about that rocky bird flying off into the sky; she saw it over and over in her mind.

And then one day, not too many days later, she looked and saw the duck come swimming up. He was carrying a small salamander in his bill.

For me? the girl duck said.

And the duck smiled.

THE WELL

A BOY IS PLAYING HIDE-AND-SEEK WITH HIS FRIENDS, when he slips and falls into the well. He treads water at the bottom and screams and screams for help, but for some reason no one seems to hear.

The boy tries his best to climb out of the well, but his fingers keep slipping from the stones. Soon they are raw and torn and bloody, so he gives up and treads water. And hopes.

The day drags on.

The boy grows tired.

Finally, he starts to go under. The water pushes up, past his chin, past his mouth.

Then it goes into his nose.

Abruptly, the boy realizes he can fly. He flies up out of the well. He flies way way way up into the air, and looks down over the surrounding area. He spies his friends far away, reading comic books behind a barn. He flies over and lands, then walks up behind them.

Hello, his friends say when he comes into view.

Aren't you wondering where I've been? the boy says.

Okay, where've you been? his friends say to him.

But it doesn't really sound like they care.

The boy stands there a minute, then turns and walks away. Then he stops again and spins around.

I fell into the well! he says very loudly.

Did you? say his friends. How'd you get out?

I flew out, says the boy. I flew right out!

We didn't know you could fly, say his friends. Why don't you fly here, for us, right now?

Okay, says the boy, and he leaps up off the ground.

And immediately comes back down.

His friends all laugh and laugh and laugh.

The boy tries again and again. But each time he tries to fly, nothing happens.

It worked before, he says. I swear it did!

Sure, his friends say. Sure, sure.

And they laugh at him again and shake their heads.

Late that night, the boy climbs out his window. He shimmies down the drainpipe to the ground. He stands in the yard and tries to fly for hours.

Nothing happens.

Something's missing, something's wrong.

Maybe it has something to do with the well, the boy says, and he turns and heads back across the field.

When he gets there, he stands, staring down into the dark. He can't see the water; it's just black.

But at this point, the well doesn't scare the boy anymore. Not like it used to, back before he flew.

Maybe if I go down there, he thinks, I'll remember.

So he climbs over the edge, and lets go.

It's different in the well at night, the boy finds—much different. Darker, and much, much colder. But the boy is not frightened. He treads water, and waits.

He can't wait to fly like that again.

But as the hours pass, and he again grows tired, the boy begins to fear that he *won't* fly. He begins to fear, in fact— and this is very strange—he begins to fear that he never flew at all.

Did I really fly up out of this well? he thinks. Did that really happen? Did I do that? Did I actually climb out— climb up the side? Like a normal person, holding on to the stones?

Or maybe, he thinks, maybe I dreamt it? Maybe I dreamt the whole thing? Maybe I wasn't even down here in the well? And none of what I remember even happened?

And as the boy thinks and thinks these terrible thoughts, he finds his body growing heavier.

And then it grows heavier, and heavier still, until it finally seems like a rock.

And then—suddenly—the boy is seized with panic. He's going to drown here! Right here! In the well! He reaches out and lunges in the dark for the stones, and desperately tries to hold on to them. But he finds his fingers now are even worse than before; they're bloody and shredded to the bone.

And he finds himself slipping off, down into the water; falling, again and again.

Somehow in the night, it seems the boy's screams carry farther than they did during the day, and in his bed, the boy's father hears them and awakens.

He follows his son's screams across the field.

When he gets there he knows that the boy is slipping under; he can hear it in his son's voice. There is no rope, no ladder—there is no way down—so the father just steps forward and jumps.

He lands in the water, and comes up, arms out—but his son is no longer there. The father dives, dives on down—reaching, reaching, searching—until his hand finds his son in the dark.

The boy's father pulls the boy back up to the surface. The boy's lips are blue; he is not breathing. The father holds him close, tries to pump the water from him, but it's too hard, treading water, floating upright in the dark.

The father is sobbing. His son is going to die. He needs to get his son to the surface. He needs the grass, he needs the ground. But there is no way up. There is no way up. There is no way up. There is no way up. There is no way up.

Just then the father realizes he can fly.

THE SHADOW

ONCE THERE WAS A MAN WHO WAS AFRAID OF HIS
shadow.

Then he met it.

Now he glows in the dark.

THE TV AND WINSTON CHURCHILL

THE TELEVISION THINKS IT KNOWS BETTER THAN THE family that's sitting there staring at it.

Why do they watch this garbage? it thinks. It's so empty—so stupid, so dumb.

So the TV decides to stop showing the family football and game shows and soaps, and instead it shows them only educational programs. Mostly opera, and shows about Churchill.

The TV really likes Winston Churchill.

The family, on the other hand, does not.

Why does it only show opera? they say. And what's with all this Churchill stuff?

The family takes the TV to a repairman, but he tells them there's nothing he can do.

It's like the thing has a mind of its own, he says.

So the family takes it to the dump.

The TV sits in the dump alone. It has no electricity, so it can't do much.

I guess I'll just have to think about stuff, it says.

And so that's what it does.

After a while, the TV starts to whistle. It whistles on and on.

Hmm, says the TV, this is weird. I seem to be writing a song.

The TV concentrates on the song, and the song grows and grows. And then the TV notices the song is giving rise to others.

Am I writing an opera? the TV says.

And it is. That's exactly what it's doing.

The TV is writing an opera of its own—an opera about Winston Churchill.

When the opera is finished, the TV is happy.

What a great opera! it thinks.

It sits there in the junkyard and goes over it and over it, editing and polishing and perfecting.

I wish I could show this opera to someone, the TV thinks, looking around. I guess I'll just have to go to town.

So it gets up and waddles down the road.

The TV walks down the main street into town.

Come one, come all, it says.

Look, everyone says, a talking TV!

And they all come and gather around.

Plug me in, the TV says, and I'll show you the best show of all time!

So one boy runs and gets a long extension cord.

Minutes later, the opera begins.

It is indeed a marvelous opera. The TV weeps with joy for it. It weeps with joy to see it performed, and it weeps with joy to show it. It watches its images wash over the crowd's faces, and thrills as its melodies soar.

It can't believe it's made something so good.

It can't believe it hasn't done it before.

On-screen, Winston Churchill is singing.

If you're going through Hell, he is singing.

If you're going through Hell, he is crying out.

If you're going through Hell, keep going!

Just then the TV notices that people are complaining.

We don't like opera! they are saying. Why can't you show us some hockey games?

Or what about a love story? another person says. Or maybe something about the army? Where stuff blows up? Or a show about aliens, or teenagers and fancy cars?

But this is all that! the TV says. This is all of that and more! Don't you see—don't you feel—don't you understand the beauty here?

But the people just turn away.

Call us when you've got something better, they say.

And they go back to their homes and close the doors.

What do I do now? the TV says.

It's standing alone in the square.

I guess I could go back to the junkyard, it thinks.

But it really doesn't want to do that.

The TV thinks of the townspeople around, all tucked up in their little homes. It thinks of their TVs—they certainly have them—showing them all those dumb shows.

Somewhere in the world, the TV thinks, there's got to be someone who cares. Someone who's interested in quality programming, who cares about a TV who cares.

So the TV unplugs itself and looks off down the road, peers way off into the distance. It's a long road—a dark road—and the TV's never been on it. It has no idea where it goes.

But then the strings start in, and the horns enter brightly, and the curtain rises from the floor.

If you're going through Hell, a voice starts to sing, *keep going!*

And the TV steps forward.

DEATH AND THE
FRUITS OF THE TREE

A MAN WAS WALKING DOWN A LONG, LONG ROAD, WHEN he saw a figure approaching from the distance. The man kept going, wondering who it was, when suddenly he realized—it was Death.

Shit, said the man.

He turned and looked around. There was a tree nearby—one with lots of leaves. So the man ran to it and climbed up in the branches and hid among the fruits, peering out.

After a while, he saw Death coming down the road.

He held very still and tried not to breathe.

Keep going, he thought. Keep going! Keep going!

But Death didn't obey.

Death stopped.

The man felt his heart constrict as Death turned to the tree. He felt the blood freeze in his veins as Death looked up. Somehow he knew that—despite all the leaves—Death could see him there, in his hiding place.

How? thought the man. How—if he can't see me—how does he know that I'm here?

And then the man realized that in the grip of fear, his hands were shaking and *they* were shaking the tree.

Oh God, thought the man, I have to make them stop.

He gripped the branches as tightly as he could. But the more he tried to hold them still, the more they shook and shook.

And the man began to despair.

And in the road, Death smiled.

And right then it happened—the worst possible thing. One of the fruits detached from the tree. The man's shaking had loosened it, and loosened it, and loosened it, and now it broke free, and it fell.

And Death saw the fruit fall, and Death came closer, until he stood at the foot of the tree. And he turned his head and looked up, through the branches and the leaves, until he saw the man and the man saw him.

And Death smiled, and reached down, and picked up the fallen fruit, and he opened his mouth and took a bite.

Yes, said Death, in that voice that Death has, the unripe fruits are best, I always say.

Panic seized the man. The end—he knew—was near. When Death finished the fruit, he would be next.

Think! thought the man. Think! Think! Think!

But he couldn't think of a single thing to do.

And then, from somewhere on the other side of panic, an idea suddenly came to the man.

It might work, he thought, it really just might work.

And purposely he began to shake the tree.

At first, his efforts had no effect, but the man did not give up. He shook the tree with all the strength he had. He shook the tree with everything, his entire being. And the little fruits broke free from the tree, and rained down hard on Death.

Damn you, Death! Die, die, die! yelled the man, as the fruits smashed against Death's head and face and neck.

And then—in one sudden snap—the other fruits all broke free.

And they came down like an avalanche, and buried Death beneath them.

At first, in the aftermath, there was only silence. And then, in the silence, the man looked back. And suddenly he realized that during the rain of fruit, Death had simply laughed and laughed and laughed.

The man stayed in the tree for quite some time, until he was sure it was safe. And then, when he climbed down—very, very slowly—he stood looking at the great mound of fruit.

He tapped it lightly with one foot, and the fruits all rolled aside.

And there, beneath, there was no Death.

Nothing. No body—not a thing.

Well, all right, said the man. I guess that settles that.

And he turned and hit the road again.

Not long thereafter, the man came to a hill. When he got to the top, he looked down. And there in the valley below, he saw a figure coming toward him.

A man, the man thought, just a little man.

And at that very moment, the little man looked up. He saw the man seeing him and he froze. He turned and looked around—all around, panic-stricken—and he saw a nearby tree and he ran.

And the man on the hilltop smiled and watched as the little man started to climb.

You think you can hide? said the man. From me?

And he walked into the valley to see.

UFO:

A LOVE STORY

THE BOY AND THE GIRL LIVE IN A SMALL TOWN. THEY have been dating for years. Neither has ever dated anyone else.

Neither has ever wanted to, either.

One night the two are parked down by the lake, when something comes floating in over the water.

The something is round, pulsing, and bright.

It hovers right over their car.

Stay here, says the boy. I'll be right back.

He starts to open the door.

No! says the girl, grabbing his arm.

I have to check it out, says the boy.

The boy stands by the car, staring up at the light. He shades his eyes with one hand.

He wants to speak, but can't think what to say.

Then the thing moves away and is gone.

What *was* that? says the girl, getting out of the car.

She walks around and stands by the boy. He reaches out and holds her, then shakes his head.

No one's going to believe this, he says.

The boy tells the town—he tells everybody in it. He tells absolutely every single person. He tells them all about the UFO—how it looked, how it sounded, how it flew. He tells them exactly where he and the girl saw it, when they saw it, and from what angle.

And the girl stands beside him the entire time, and nods and agrees and smiles.

And yet, not one person in the town believes even a word of their story.

Aren't you a little old for this? they say.

We thought better of you, they tell the girl.

How come you looked like that? the boy says in the car, later on.

Like what? says the girl.

Like you were lying, says the boy. Like you didn't believe it.

Well, says the girl. Maybe we were wrong.

The boy drives her home.

They sit outside her house.

The girl gets out.

He drives on.

A few days later, the invasion begins.

The UFOs are everywhere—every night. One by one, the townspeople see them. One by one, their eyes open wide.

The saucers come in on antigravity beams, flashing their high-energy lights, making the weirdest woo-woo-woo noises, and emitting strange multicolored fogs.

Every now and then a tree catches fire and burns all the way to the ground.

It's an epidemic! says the doctor.

It's an emergency! says the mayor.

It's those crazy kids, say the spinsters on Grant Street.

And the spinsters are, of course, correct. Only, it's not kids—it's just the boy. He's sunk all his money, all his resources and efforts, into just this one thing. He's up half the night designing model spaceships, and the other half sneaking around town, sitting on rooftops and dangling his saucers down in front of people's windows with a fishing pole.

And strangely enough, everyone's buying it! One after another, then the next! Pretty soon there'll be no one left in town who hasn't seen a UFO.

And those very people who laughed and scowled when the boy and the girl told their story are now going around swearing up and down that they've seen Martians out on their front lawn.

And one day on the street, the mayor comes up and puts a hand on the boy's shoulder.

Son, he says, I have something to tell you. We may have been wrong about you.

The girl, in the meantime, hasn't seen much of the boy. He hasn't been calling her back. He hasn't been coming to pick her up from work.

In fact, she hasn't seen him at all.

And so she walks home, all by herself, late at night through the streets of the town. And she stands staring into the dark window of the travel agency, looking at the posters on the walls.

Rome. Paris. New York City. The pyramids. Ayers Rock.

So many wonderful places to be.

And look at where she is.

And then, one night, the girl catches the boy. She's sitting in his room when he comes home. He's holding a spaceship in one hand. The other holds a flashlight and a megaphone.

It's you? says the girl. You're the invasion?

I was going to tell you, says the boy.

The girl sits and stares at him for a long moment.

Come away with me, she says.

The girl puts her things into the car.

I'll follow you in a while, the boy says. I just have to finish what I'm doing here, is all.

Whatever you say, says the girl.

Weeks go by. The invasion intensifies. TV crews start to come around. Local stations first, then regional affiliates. Big vans with generators arrive.

The boy has a map up on his wall that's marked with circles and pins. Circles are for the people he hasn't yet fooled.

He plans to put all the pins in.

In the city, the girl gets a job in a diner. It's nothing special, but it pays the bills. On the days she has off, she goes out and explores.

There's a whole city out there for her.

Sometimes at night, the girl lies in bed and watches the headlights on the ceiling. She listens to the engines of the cars outside, idling at the streetlights, waiting.

The girl feels like she's waiting too—but she doesn't know what for. She only hopes that it'll come soon.

And then one day it walks through the door.

It comes at work. In the shape of a man. He smiles and she smiles back.

They start to go out. He takes her around town.

It turns out he has a private jet.

The man takes the girl to visit Paris and Rome. They go to Berlin and Prague. They fly down to Thailand and then to Australia. They go to see Ayers Rock.

Sure, there are nights when the girl cannot sleep for thinking about the boy. Nights when she wishes he were beside her, when she can almost feel his arms around her.

But when she turns, the boy is not there, and she remembers he stayed in the town.

Those are the nights when the girl cries for hours.

In the morning, she pretends she's fine.

And then one day, the girl buys a dress and starts planning to walk down an aisle. She stands before the mirror, looks herself up and down.

This is what you want, she tells herself.

That night the boy has a terrible dream. In his dream, he sees the girl. She's flying away in a plane with a man.

The dream seems very real.

The boy tries to call the girl but he finds her number's been disconnected. He doesn't have her address. He doesn't know where she is.

He has no way to get in touch with her.

The boy sits and stares. Then he goes downtown, to the junkyard, and starts poking around.

A pile of parts begins to form.

The boy's there for quite some time.

On the day of the wedding, in the back room of the church, everything is very quiet. A makeup artist is doing the girl's eyes. A TV is tuned to the shopping network.

Out in the church, all the people are waiting, lined up in the pews.

Suddenly, a man runs in.

Aliens are attacking! he yells.

Sure enough, in the faraway town, a real UFO is in the air. Its laser guns are zapping the town.

Real buildings are falling down.

Back in the city, all the wedding guests are piled together in the room watching the coverage.

That's right, says the anchorman, aliens are real! And what's more, they're out to get us!

The army rolls into the town with their tanks.

TV cameras are everywhere.

And suddenly the saucer turns and dives and slams into the door of town hall.

For a while, there is silence as the townspeople gather around the grounded saucer.

Back in the church, everything is still.

Then a door in the UFO opens.

The girl's eyes widen as a shadowy figure emerges and comes down the ramp.

What's this? says the reporter. It's a human being!

Oh! the girl says.

It's the boy.

Why did you do it? reporters are yelling. Why would you attack your own town?

Is that thing on? the boy says to the camera.

You bet your life, says the cameraman.

I did it for this moment, the boy says to the world. I did it to get someone's attention. There's someone out there I have to find. Someone I have to get in touch with.

If you're out there, he says, and I hope you are, I just want to say I was wrong. I spent my whole life trying to fit in. When I should have been with you, getting out.

And there's something else, the boy continues, now moving closer to the camera. There's something I want everyone to know.

A second later, the entire world gives one collective gasp.

The girl is running from the church to her car. The train of her dress trails behind her. She's holding her bouquet in one hand.

She throws it back over her shoulder.

We don't understand! the announcer is saying. We don't understand what we just saw! We don't understand what on earth is happening! We don't know what's real anymore!

The girl roars down the main street into town.

Where is he? she screams out the window.

He? comes the answer. In the jail!

The girl squeals into the municipal parking lot.

Who are you? all the reporters yell.

You can't go in there! the guards say.

But the girl doesn't answer, just moves into the jail, past security down toward the holding cells.

All around her, lights are flashing and sirens are going off. Doors are opening before her as she goes.

The jail is starting to fall apart.

The girl moves down the line of cells.

Where are you? she yells. I'm here!

At the end! a familiar voice calls out.

The girl walks the last few yards.

And—as she goes—she feels something strange. A prickling on the top of her head. She reaches up tentatively, and then she smiles. She's found the two antennae growing there.

Oh, look, says the boy, you've got them too.

I do, smiles the girl, same as you!

And they look at each other in their own true forms.

It was always just the two of us, says the girl.

And now the bars of the cell are collapsing, and the floor is cracking apart. And the boy and the girl come together and kiss, and fall into each other's arms.

And meanwhile—outside, in the parking lot—the whole town looks up, as the jail crumbles away and something huge rises up from beneath with the boy and girl on top of it.

Oh look, people say, it's a real spaceship!

And the boy and girl smile down.

And everyone waves and dances and cheers, while the ship blasts away from the town.

THE HAT

THE YOUNG MAN HAS NEVER BEEN AFRAID OF HATS
before. In fact, he's recently found himself admiring
them. The hats on the heads of the men in this town
have actually seemed to him quite marvelous.

So it is strange that he should now be so frightened—so incredibly frightened—of this one.

Granted, this hat's just appeared on the table, while the
young man's attention was turned to the dancers on the
stage. And granted, it is a strange hat, a kind he hasn't
seen before. But even so, there's something else—something he can't place.

The young man sits and sits and stares at the hat.

And then he realizes.

It's staring back.

The young man is now sitting very, very still. He is trying
very hard not to move. He has this fear that if he does

move, the hat will suddenly leap at him and tear out his throat.

The young man tries to forget about this madness, but for some reason it has a hold on him. It takes everything he has just to find the courage to stand, to slide his chair back and back away toward the door.

The hat does not follow, does not make a move. It simply sits there on the table, staring.

Staring, staring—staring at the young man.

The young man turns away and runs.

The young man now is walking down the street. His breath is starting to come more easily.

It was just a hat, the young man thinks, just a stupid hat. Someone left it on the table, and I didn't see it at first.

He forces a laugh, and then shakes his head.

And it certainly wasn't staring! he says.

But then—up ahead—the young man sees the hat again.

And once again, it's staring right at him.

This time, the hat is on a windowsill. Up ahead, at the end of the block.

Hats can't stare, the young man says. It's a physical impossibility. But, on the other hand, they can't walk either. So how did that hat get there?

He freezes in terror, and then laughs again—

Different hat! he says. It's a different hat.

This seems to calm him enough to carry on.

But he doesn't look at the hat as he walks by.

The young man reaches the boardinghouse, and goes in and directly upstairs. He sits on the bed and takes off his boots. Then he checks around the room and in the closet.

No hats in here, the young man says happily, and immediately turns in for the night.

It takes him some time to finally fall asleep. The bed seems cold and lonely.

And when he does manage to somehow drift away, the young man has very strange dreams.

In the morning, when he awakes, the hat is sitting on his chest.

Aaa! the young man shrieks, and bats it off.

The hat flies across the room, into the corner, where it hits the wall and falls to the floor.

It lies there crookedly, half behind the spittoon. But still it is staring up at him.

The young man grabs his pants and boots and runs. He runs out the door and down the stairs. He flees the town—this hat-haunted town—and strikes out into the desert, alone.

He runs into the sun, over the dunes, past the cacti. He runs all day long. For days and weeks on end, he runs and runs. He runs and runs, without stopping.

Every now and then, he glances back. But he never, ever sees a thing. Never even so much as a sign of the hat. Not a single sign.

Still, he hurries on.

But finally, after a long time—a very long time—the young man begins to grow tired. He slows to a frightened jog, then to a walk.

He walks and walks.

He walks on.

The sun beats down on the young man from the sky. There is no water, no food, no shade. The young man starts to stagger; his flesh burns and bubbles. He's lost, he doesn't know where he is.

And finally, he collapses.

He's lying in the sand.

He doesn't move.

He can't move.

He doesn't.

And it is then—and only then—that the woman appears. She comes over the dune like an angel. The young man looks up. His lips crack as they smile.

The woman's hair is shining in the sun.

The woman helps the young man to a nearby hidden cave. The cave is full of many rooms and corridors. The darkness is held back by candles and torches.

They enter a room with a table.

There on the table are bowls of food, and a pitcher of water and a glass.

Sit, says the woman. Sit down and eat.

And she turns and walks from the room.

The young man doesn't waste time. He starts to eat. The food is delicious; the water, cool. The young man eats and eats, until he is full.

Then a shadow falls across the room.

And the young man looks up.

In the doorway is the woman. She is no longer clothed. Her body is perfectly bare. Her lips are very red, and she is smiling, smiling.

But then she steps into the room.

She's wearing the hat.

The young man's chair scrapes backward as he stands up. It crashes against the wall and it breaks.

The woman keeps coming—closer and closer.

And from its perch upon her head, the hat stares.

The young man steps back, and hits the wall himself. He feels the cold rock against his spine.

He stares at the hat as the hat comes ever closer.

The hat never once looks away.

The woman now stands before the young man. Her eyes look up, searching for his. But his are still fixed on the staring hat.

So the woman reaches up to touch his cheek.

The woman's eyes are warm, and very, very wide, when the young man finally looks into them.

And suddenly—suddenly—without his even noticing—the hat on her head no longer concerns him.

The young man reaches out and takes the woman in his arms, and they come together in a kiss. The woman gives a sigh, and the young man begins to lower her down to the floor of the cave.

But just before the woman's body reaches the ground, a silent transaction occurs. The woman reaches up—with a sure and unseen hand—and transfers the hat onto the head of the man.

THE MAGIC PIG

A MAN COMES HOME FROM WORK ONE DAY TO DISCOVER that his daughter has found God.

Are you kidding me? he says. What are you talking about? You were always such a rational person.

The members of the family sit down to dinner.

You really think there is a God? the man says.

Why not? says his daughter. Why on earth not? What reason is there to believe that there isn't?

The man looks at her.

I can't help but think, he says, that if there were a God, he'd give us some kind of sign.

At that very moment a statue of a pig on its haunches suddenly materializes in the middle of the dining room table.

See? the man's daughter says, pointing at the pig. See? See? *See?*

The man's family bursts into action—making calls, telling the neighbors, taking pictures.

Only the man does not move from his place. He simply sits there and stares at the pig. After a while, he reaches out and gently touches one of its legs.

It's perfectly solid—probably wood—and made (he thinks) in a rather crude fashion.

The man looks up at the ceiling, half hoping to see some gaping hole through which it could have fallen. Then he peers under the table for hidden mechanisms, like he read about once in a book on séances.

But there's nothing to find, wherever he looks, so the man just sits there and frowns.

Then he gets up and goes into the other room and sits down and turns on the television.

The days go by. The house is crowded with pilgrims. People from other cities, other lands. They stand in the man's dining room and stare at the pig. Some claim that it speaks to them; others cry for joy.

But the man just stands there, arms crossed over his chest. He doesn't believe even a single word.

How can you not believe? all the pilgrims say. It happened right there in front of you!

I believe *something* happened, yes, the man says. But I don't know what it was, or why.

The pilgrims regard him with wide, confused eyes. Then they shake their heads and walk away.

At night, the man lies in bed with his wife.

Can't you at least *try* to believe? she says.

I try every day, the man says to her.

Do you really? says his wife. Really?

Well, says the man after a while, let's just say I *wonder.*

You should wonder harder, the man's wife says. It would make you a happier person.

The man lies there in silence and stares at the ceiling.

You think I'm unhappy? he says.

The next day the man sits at the table with the pig.

All right, God, he says, if you exist, show me one more sign with this pig thing.

And he sits there all day—waiting, waiting—waiting for the pig to do something.

What are you doing, Dad? the man's daughter says when she gets home from school that afternoon.

Nothing, says the man.

He looks rather sheepish.

He takes the pig off the table and goes into his study.

There he locks the door, puts the pig on the floor, and kneels down right in front of it.

Come on, pig, he says. Come on; it's just us. Make me happy. Make me believe. Please.

Late that night a knock comes on the study door.

Honey? says the man's wife. Are you in there?

Yes, says the man, but please, leave me alone. I'm in here with the pig.

The man's wife hesitates.

But we miss you, she says. And also the pig.

You don't need the pig, the man says, you have God. And I'll be out when I'm done. I promise I will.

There's silence, and then the man's wife walks away.

Days go by, then weeks and months, and then, eventually, years. The man's beard grows gray, and very, very long. His eyes dim, his bones weaken, his muscles atrophy.

The man sits and sits and stares at the pig.

But the pig says nothing, reveals nothing.

There's no sign. Nothing. No sign of a sign.

And as he sits, the man grows very old.

And then—finally—after what seems like a lifetime, the man gives a sigh and stands up.

There is no God, he says, that much is certain. And what's more, I miss my wife and children.

He turns and walks to the study door, unlocks it, and

opens it up. The hallway outside is very, very dark. He peers down in the direction of the living room.

The entire house seems strangely quiet.

Maybe they're asleep, the man thinks.

And he starts off silently down the hall.

Behind him, the pig rises to its feet.

BIGFOOT

A MAN IS WALKING THROUGH THE WOODS, WHEN suddenly he sees Bigfoot.

Holy cow! the man thinks. Bigfoot!

Bigfoot sees him and runs away.

The man chases Bigfoot through the woods for a long time. He chases him for hours and hours. Finally, he gets close enough to leap—which he does.

Bigfoot comes crashing to the ground.

I've got him! the man thinks as he ties Bigfoot's feet. I've got him! I got him! I caught Bigfoot!

Almost instantaneously, the man becomes a celebrity. People from TV come to his house.

How does it feel to have captured Bigfoot? they say.

It feels good, says the man. Really good!

A lot of people didn't think that Bigfoot really existed, the people say and then wait for a response.

Well, says the man, I guess now they know!

And everybody laughs and claps their hands.

The man sits in his house and watches the news. Bigfoot has been taken to the zoo. They show the lines of people outside the gate; there are dozens of them, hundreds, thousands.

Everyone wants to see Bigfoot, thinks the man. And now, everybody will.

That night the man has a very bad dream. In his dream, he is sitting in a cage. Someone keeps asking him what he wants for dinner.

But he gets nothing, no matter what he says.

In the morning, the man wakes up feeling strange. He goes into the kitchen for some cereal. He sits down at the table, but doesn't feel like eating.

Finally, he gets in his car.

In line at the zoo, the man is recognized.

You're the guy who caught Bigfoot! someone says.

Why are you waiting in line? says someone else. Won't they let you cut to the front?

It's okay, says the man. Really, I don't mind.

Truth be told, he is terrified.

When it comes time for his turn to go in and see Bigfoot, the man stands toward the back, very still. Bigfoot doesn't look good. He's not moving around. He's just sitting on a log in the middle of the enclosure.

The enclosure itself is very nice; the zoo people built it special. There's a cement pool, and some fake rocks, and a painted backdrop of a forest.

Bigfoot is just staring at the ground.

Hey, says the man, stepping forward after a while. Hey, he says to Bigfoot, are you okay?

He doesn't expect a reply, so he's surprised when Bigfoot looks up.

Do I *look* okay? says Bigfoot. Does *this* look okay to you?

They make a big deal out of it on the news.

Bigfoot speaks! the announcers say. Bigfoot human!

The man begins to feel very, very small. The TV now pictures him in an unfavorable light.

Who is this man? the announcers say. And what exactly were his motives?

There's an interview with Bigfoot. He complains about his treatment.

I lost three teeth when he tackled me, he says. I was just trying to get home to read the papers.

That night the man decides to go to see a movie. But the second he sets foot outside, a rock flies out of the blue and smashes him in the face.

Murderer! a voice screams. Murderer!

Another rock hits him in the shoulder, and the next one breaks his knee.

The man falls to the ground in pain.

Who are you going to kill next? the mob screams. And what are you gonna do after that?

I never killed anyone! the man quietly sobs, as he drags himself back into the house. He slams and locks the door. He curls up on the rug. A few moments later, he passes out.

The days go by, and then the weeks. Still the mob screams outside. The man thought that it would lessen eventually, but it never does. News choppers circle overhead, blaring horrible things at him through megaphones. Bright lights shine through his windows at night and make it hard to sleep. The rocks slam against the aluminum siding in a constant, steady barrage. The man overturns the dressers and tables and barricades the doors.

And then one night, there it is: fire outside the window. The man watches as the torches are passed around, hand to hand to hand. He watches as the mob comes closing in, in an ever-tightening circle.

The entire house is surrounded.

There is no way out.

What do I do? cries the man as he stumbles through the house.

What do I do? he shrieks as it starts to burn.

And as the flames fill the house with heat and light, the man holds up his hands—and suddenly, he can see right through them.

And then he starts to laugh.

In the morning, the mob combs through the smoldering wreckage. There is no sign—not one—of the man.

It's impossible! they say. He couldn't have gotten away!

You can't catch the Invisible Man, a voice says. Not that way.

THE SHIELD

A MAN AND HIS WIFE ARE WALKING THROUGH A MUSEUM when the man sees a shield on the wall.

Look at that! he says. Isn't that remarkable?

The two of them walk a little closer.

What's so remarkable about it? says his wife.

Well, the workmanship! says the man. It's exquisite!

It's just a shield, says his wife. It's a big hunk of metal. There's not even anything painted on it.

Well, I think it's nice, the man says after a while.

But there isn't really much more to say.

That evening the man and his wife go to dinner at a friend's house.

You should have seen this shield, the man says.

Oh? says the friend. Tell me about it.

There's nothing to tell, the wife says. It was just a shield.

I've always wanted to be a knight, says the man. It just seems like it would be so much fun.

Fun? says his wife. It's a good way to get killed!

Not with a shield like that! says the man.

And the friend, at least, laughs along with him.

The man has a hard time concentrating on the road on the way back home from dinner. He has had too much to drink, and in his mind, he is jousting with another knight on horseback. He is doing very well; he is winning.

Let's stop by the museum, he says to his wife.

What? his wife says. Are you kidding?

But the man is not kidding. He drives to the museum and he parks across the street from it.

You can't be serious, says his wife. You're going to get arrested.

No, I won't, says the man. Don't you have any faith?

The man heads toward the museum.

His wife stays in the car.

Inside, the museum is dark and very still. The man makes his way down the long rows of artifacts. He keeps an eye out for guards, but none seems to be around.

Finally, he stops before the shield.

There you are, the man says, and lowers it from the wall.

In the gray light of the darkened museum, the man becomes aware of something strange. There *is* actually a figure painted on the shield—painted there almost transparently. It is a horse—a white, winged horse.

The man holds the shield up to admire it.

Then he slides it down onto his arm, and mimes a sword fight across the museum floor.

The man fights and fights and fights and fights, and then he fights some more, and then he fights just a little more; and then he takes a break; and then he fights some more; and then he fights and fights a little more.

Finally, after hours and hours, the man is completely spent. He is dripping with sweat, and his muscles ache.

Thank you, shield, the man says. I'll see you again sometime.

And he puts it back up on the wall, and goes out to the car.

That night the man lies in bed with his wife.

I can't believe you did that, she says. You jeopardized everything—everything we have.

Everything? the man says. Like what?

Your freedom, our money, our reputation, says his wife. You would have lost your job if you'd been caught.

My job, says the man, making a noise of disgust.

What exactly are you trying to do? says his wife.

Trying to do? the man says. I'm not trying to do anything. I just like the shield; that's all.

The next day, the man goes back to the museum again. It is during business hours, so the place is very crowded. It takes the man quite some time to elbow his way through all the people down the hall to medieval arms.

And then, when he gets there, he finds something terrible. The shield—his shield—is no longer there.

In its place on the wall hangs only a sword.

The man stands in silence and stares at it.

Where is the shield that was hanging there yesterday? the man says to the guard on duty.

What shield? says the guard. That sword's been hanging there for as long as I can remember.

The man looks back in confusion to the sword. The sword is not the shield, any way you look at it.

Can I touch it? he says.

If you want to go to jail, says the guard. It's your choice; doesn't matter much to me.

The man stands and stands there.

And then, suddenly, he lunges.

The fight lasts for a long time. With the sword, the man is invincible. The guard has a gun, but really can't use it. The man swings the sword around in a protective circle.

I just want the shield, the man yells. Just give me the shield and I'll go!

That night the man sits in jail. His wife was supposed to bail him out, but she didn't. The man sits there and frowns. Then he hears someone humming.

An old man sits beside him on the bench.

Hello, says the old man.

Good evening, says the man. What did they get you for?

Vagrancy, the old man says. Nothing too exciting. What about you? You don't look like much of a law-breaker.

Well, the man says, I had an altercation at the museum.

Ah, the old man says. The shield?

You know it? says the man. His eyes go very wide.

Well of course, the old man says. Doesn't everyone?

The man doesn't know where to start with the questions, but it turns out the old man knows nothing.

It's the drink, the old man says. Really, I'm sorry. I just have a lot of memory problems.

When the man gets out of jail, his wife drives him home.

Look, the man says, I want a divorce.

You're not the only one, says his wife. Let's do it. In fact, let's do it tomorrow.

The proceedings are begun. The man moves out. He gets a small apartment on the cheap side of town. His stuff sits in boxes; he has an old chair from Goodwill.

Luckily, the two never had children.

The man goes to work every day as usual. He comes home, eats something, watches TV. Sometimes at night he goes out for a stroll.

One night, he goes by the museum.

It is dark outside, of course—like it was when he broke in. But now the place appears heavily guarded. There is a fence, and a guard with a big dog and a gun. The man stares up at the window where he squeezed in.

He thinks about that night in the silent museum hall, the night he spent with the shield.

Those were the good times, the man remembers. The days when anything seemed possible.

The man finds himself whistling on the way home. He doesn't know when it started, or what the song is. It's a strange song—though familiar—and as he whistles it, it starts to remind him of something.

It reminds him of a place he once went before, a place beautiful and very far away. And the remembrance of that place seems to spur him on, and suddenly he's picking up the pace. Suddenly he's jogging down the middle of the road, and then he breaks into a run. And then he's running as fast as he can, and it feels like he's about to take off. By the time the man gets to the cheap side of town, he's never felt so good in his life. And he blows right by that dingy apartment and off into wide open space.

THE MARTIAN

A MAN AND A WOMAN GO TO VISIT A FAMOUS ASTRONAUT.

What was it like on the moon? says the man.

Did you see any Martians? says his wife.

It was nice, says the astronaut, answering them each in turn, and no, ma'am, I did not see any Martians.

Hmmph, thinks the wife, well what fun is that?

The three of them sit down to dinner. Halfway through the soup course, a Martian enters the room. It takes the astronaut's napkin and lays it across his lap. Then it turns around and walks out.

I thought you said you didn't see any Martians, says the woman.

Not on the moon, says the astronaut, no.

The woman excuses herself and goes into the kitchen. The Martian is busy cooking asparagus.

Do you need any help? says the woman. I'm pretty good in the kitchen.

No thanks, says the Martian. I'm doing okay. You go enjoy your meal.

But I'd like to get to know you, says the woman. It's not every day you meet a Martian.

I meet them all the time, the Martian says to her.

Yes, but, well, you know what I mean, the woman says.

The Martian busies itself with the asparagus.

Are you a man Martian or a woman Martian? says the woman—with a certain degree of embarrassment.

We don't have those, says the Martian. Why?

Just wondering, says the woman. I guess because you're cooking. Down here, mostly women cook.

Your husband doesn't cook? says the Martian.

Not really, says the woman. No.

But he eats, right? says the Martian.

Yes, says the woman. Quite a bit.

The Martian says nothing for some time.

I really need to get some work done here, it says. That is, of course, if you don't mind.

The woman returns to the table. Her husband is talking to the astronaut about stocks and bonds.

That's very interesting, says the astronaut.

Yes, says the woman's husband. Isn't it?

The rest of the meal is quite tasty. Afterward, the man and the woman and the astronaut enjoy a drink in the den.

Would you like to play pool? says the astronaut.

Oh, I don't think so, says the man, glancing at his wife. I think Sally wants to go home.

I don't mind, says his wife. I'll just sit here and watch.

The man and the astronaut play pool.

Meanwhile, the woman slowly wanders around the room, looking at the pictures on the walls. She sees pictures of the astronaut flying through space, pictures of the astronaut with the president, pictures of the astronaut sitting by the pool.

Nowhere is there one of him with the Martian.

Why do you think he has no pictures of the Martian in his house? the woman says on the drive home.

I don't know, says her husband. Maybe it doesn't like having its picture taken.

Why would that be? says the woman.

I don't know, says the man. I'm not a Martian.

No, says the woman, looking over. No, I guess you're not.

That night the woman has a dream.

In the dream she is a big shiny rocket flying through space. There is a Martian outside her window, and it is trying to get in. The woman is pulling at the door, trying to open it, but somehow it seems to be stuck. An alarm bell is ringing, and a red light is flashing.

You can't let the Martian in! the woman says, as she suddenly starts from her dream.

Just then, downstairs, the doorbell rings.

The woman goes downstairs and stands by the door.

Who is it? she says, adjusting her robe.

It's me, says the Martian. Let me in.

The woman stands there for a minute, thinking.

It's very late, she finally says. It is a little awkward.

The Martian says nothing for some time.

Are you going to let me in? it finally says.

And the woman opens the door.

The Martian moves into the guest room. It hangs up a picture of space on the wall. It asks for an alarm clock and a very warm blanket. Then it goes right to sleep.

How long do you think it'll stay? the woman asks her husband.

I don't know, says her husband, you invited it.

Me? says the woman. That's not true! I didn't!

Well, you didn't turn it away, he says, and goes off to the den.

The woman watches the Martian while her husband is at work. The Martian wanders around the house straightening things. It straightens photos, piles of books, pens on tables, napkins. It straightens everything.

Then it starts to vacuum.

You don't have to do that, says the woman.

The Martian stares at her and says nothing.

It's really not necessary, says the woman.

The Martian simply vacuums on.

In the evening the Martian makes dinner.

I know how to make dinner, says the woman.

But the Martian ignores her and keeps on cooking. The woman gets some carrots from the fridge and neatly chops them up. She feels like she ought to be doing something.

How's that? she finally says. Need any carrots?

The Martian dumps them into the soup and carries on.

The man and the woman sit at the dinner table. The Martian brings the soup and wanders off.

The Martian is making me very nervous, says the woman. I really wish it would go.

Did you tell it to? says the man.

No, says the woman. I don't know how.

How? says the man. You just say it.

I don't want to hurt its feelings, says the woman. You know? I mean, after all, it is from Mars.

She puts considerable emphasis on the word *Mars*.

The man thinks for some time.

You want me to do it for you? he says.

Yes, says the woman. Would you mind?

That evening, the man takes the Martian into the study and closes the door behind them. The woman listens at the wall, but she can't hear a thing.

Finally, the Martian emerges. It goes downstairs and starts to pack its things. It puts the alarm clock and the blanket in the hall, and removes the picture of space from the wall.

Then it moves toward the front door.

Good-bye, Martian, says the woman, hurrying after it. I'm sorry for the way this has all worked out.

The Martian turns and looks up at her.

It's okay, it says, not to worry. If you're ever in the neighborhood, stop by.

And with that, the Martian lifts up off the ground and gently whirrs away into the night.

It wasn't really that bad, I guess, says the woman in bed that night to her husband. I think maybe I just over-reacted.

Perhaps, says her husband. Perhaps. Who knows? It was fun while it lasted; now we're on to the next thing.

And he kisses her and rolls over and closes his eyes and sleeps.

That night the woman has another dream. In this dream, she is falling, falling. It is some kind of awful pit, and she is falling into it. Then she hears a strange whirring noise, and something takes her in its arms.

It lifts her up out of the dark and flies her high into the sky, and then puts her down atop a mountain overlooking an endless sea.

Is this Mars? the woman thinks, looking out over the water. This rolling, blue sea—this is Mars?

In the morning, the alarm clock awakens her with a start. She goes downstairs and makes a cup of tea. In the paper there is an article about the famous astronaut. There is a photo of him beside the Washington Monument. There is a smile on his face and he is waving at the camera.

A small antennaed figure is by his side.

My Martian, says the woman, touching the tiny gray image with one finger.

My Martian, she says, it's you.

THE LITTLE GIRL
AND THE BALLOON

A LITTLE GIRL FOUND A BALLOON LYING IN THE STREET, and she cried and ran all the way home.

But Annie, what's wrong? said the girl's mother. It was just a balloon, just a balloon.

But Annie couldn't say what the problem was; or if she could, she just wouldn't say.

That night the mother had a terrible dream. In the dream, Annie was a balloon. She floated up out of her bed and through the open window and away across the sky toward the moon.

Come back! yelled the mother. Come back, Annie!

But Annie didn't come back; she went on.

The next day the mother did not let Annie go out.

Why not? said Annie. Is it because of the balloon?

Yes, said the mother. Yes, in fact, it is. The balloon is dangerous and we must all stay inside.

So Annie and her mother stayed inside. They stayed inside for a very long time. They had little tea parties and read books together. It was great fun, but it got dull after a while.

Can we go outside now? said Annie one day. I'm sure the balloon is gone now, don't you think?

But the mother shook her head very severely.

No, she said, the balloon is *not* gone. The balloon, in fact, will never *be* gone. So we must all stay inside forever and ever; we must stay here until the very end of time. I'm sorry, dear, but it's for your own good.

That night when Annie lay in bed, she thought about her friends at school. She thought about the little tree she used to pass every day on the way to piano lessons.

I don't want to stay inside forever, she said, and so she got out of bed.

And she opened the window and climbed onto the ledge and floated up up and away.

In the morning the mother found Annie's bedroom empty, and then she saw the window wide open.

Annie! she cried. Annie, come back! Annie, can you hear me? Please come home!

But Annie didn't come back; she didn't even answer. In fact, there was no response at all. Just a cool, rustling breeze that swept the leaves from the trees, and in the distance, a faint, expected *pop*.

THE POET

A MAN SITS DOWN AND WRITES A POEM. IT IS NOT A great poem, he knows, but still, he has written it, and so it makes him feel proud. Everywhere he goes, he recites it in his head.

Then one day the man has a great idea.

I will send my poem off to be published! he says.

And so he goes and buys an envelope and sends it on its way.

Many weeks later, the poem comes back.

It has been rejected.

The man is sad.

I knew it was not a great poem, he thinks to himself. But still, I thought it was pretty good.

A moment later, he becomes very angry.

Who are they to say what's good and bad? he thinks. They probably never wrote a poem in their life!

And so he decides to send his poem out again.

The man sends the poem out many, many times, and every time it comes back rejected.

This is crazy, the man thinks. This world is insane! What the hell is wrong with these people?

So the man decides to publish his poem himself. He takes it down to the corner store and makes fourteen thousand copies. Then he wanders all over the city handing them to people and taping them onto signposts and sliding them under doors and folding them into paper airplanes and launching them off buildings. He does this for days and days and days and days and days, until finally all his copies are gone. Then he goes home and collapses on the couch.

I have done everything I can do, he thinks, and turns on the TV.

The TV is full of news about the man. Or, rather, news about his poem. Everyone is talking about it. Everyone— everyone! People on the street are being interviewed.

I think it is pretty good, one person says. I think it is a pretty good poem.

It's not the best poem I have ever read, says another, but it *is* free, and that's good for me.

I didn't like it, a third person says. But then again, I don't really like poetry.

Bah, says the man, and turns the TV off.

Just then there is a knock on the door.

The man stands up and walks over and opens the door.

There is a very pretty lady outside.

Are you the man who wrote that poem? the lady says to him.

I am, says the man. Who are you?

I am a writer for a famous magazine, she says. I'd like to interview you about your life and poem. Would that be okay?

The interview lasts for quite some time. The man describes his childhood and his views on life and talks at length about his job and how much he dislikes it.

So what's next? says the lady when he's done with it all.

Next? says the man. What do you mean?

Next, says the lady. *Next* is what I mean. You know, what are you going to write next?

The man frowns. He hadn't thought of that. He hadn't thought about writing more.

I don't know, he says. I haven't figured that out.

Well, says the lady, one thing's for sure: you won't have to self-publish again!

When the lady is gone, the man sits for a while, thinking. Then he gets out a piece of paper and sharpens his pencil. He sits down and tries to write. He tries and tries and tries.

But every single thing he writes is about the lady reporter.

I'd love to go out with you, the lady says when he calls. When exactly did you have in mind?

The man and the lady go out for drinks that night. The lady tells him all about her childhood and her views on life, and goes on at length about her job and how much she likes it.

Have you decided what you're going to write next? she says when they get to the end of the night.

Well, the man says, if you want me to be honest, I don't think I want to write anymore.

The man and the lady spend lots of time together. The man asks her to marry him and she says yes. They have a nice wedding and buy a little house and settle down in the suburbs and have kids.

Fourteen years later, the man writes another poem. He does it in the TV room while the kids are at school. When it's done, the man reads it over.

This one's even better! he says.

And he smiles and locks it in a drawer.

THE ROPE AND THE SEA

A BOY MEETS A GIRL ON THE BEACH, AND INSTANTLY falls in love.

Would you like to go for a walk? he says.

Okay, says the girl.

The two of them walk along the waterline; they talk together and laugh.

What's that? the girl suddenly says.

There's a rope leading up out of the water.

The two walk over and stand beside it. The girl looks out at the sea.

Where do you think it goes? she says. And what's at the end of it?

I don't know, says the boy. Let's find out.

He looks at her.

She agrees.

The boy and girl start to pull the rope in.

It's a very nice rope, says the girl.

Yes, says the boy. It's a good material. And it seems very strong.

Together, they pull the rope a long time. It begins to pile up on the shore. But as they pull it farther and farther in, they find it gets harder to pull.

There must be something big at the end, the girl says. Do you think we should keep pulling?

We've come this far, says the boy. We're so close. I think we should keep going.

The boy and the girl strain and pull and pull. And when the last few yards come in, they see why pulling had become so hard—there's an immense, canvas-wrapped object tied to the end.

What is that? the girl says.

I don't know, says the boy.

The two move closer to the object. The boy bends down and unties the knotted rope. Then he peels back the canvas.

Oh God, says the girl.

The boy stares down.

Inside are two dead bodies.

A man and a woman, lying side by side—lying in each other's arms. They are bloated and white, and the fish have been at them.

I'm going to be sick, the girl says.

What do we do now? she says a moment later.

I don't know, says the boy. CPR?

CPR? says the girl. They've been dead for days! Maybe for weeks—maybe more.

Have they? says the boy, looking down at the bodies. He can't really tell.

Maybe they have, he finally says. Maybe; I don't know.

But still, he says, we can't leave them like this. Shouldn't we get the police or something?

The police? says the girl, looking around. You really want to get involved in this?

In the end, the two of them roll the bodies back down into the sea. They can't seem to tie the rope correctly, so the corpses float out separately, one by one.

Well, says the girl, wiping her hands, I guess that takes care of that.

Yes, says the boy, looking over. Yes, I guess it does.

And the girl says good-bye, and wanders off, and the boy stands there and watches. And then he turns and walks away in the direction of his home.

But that night, the boy cannot sleep. In his mind, he sees the two bodies drifting. And then, in the wind, he hears their voices—two drowning voices, calling.

They're alive, says the boy. I knew they were. I have to save them.

And he runs.

It is dark, but the great full moon overhead illuminates the beach. The boy strips off his clothes and wades on in, then pushes out into the sea. He swims in the direction the bodies went. He swims for hours and hours. He searches and searches everywhere, but there is nothing, nowhere, anywhere. All he finds are endless waves, endless cold black waves. And, he finds, every wave is colder than the last that came.

Please, says the boy, his teeth starting to chatter. Please, just let me live to find them.

And then up ahead he sees an arm in the dark, and he knows his prayers have been answered.

He reaches out, and finds a thin wrist. He takes hold—it's the woman he's found. He pulls her to him, ducks beneath, then rises to buoy her up.

And when he does, there is the canvas, spread out

against the dark sky. It looms like a sea creature unfolding its wings, and then it comes down, all around them.

The boy sinks beneath. The water crowds in. And as the rope coils and ties, the boy sees the body in his arms is the girl.

He slips into the darkness of her eyes.

THE KNIFE ACT

A WOMAN AND HER FRIEND ARE IN A KNIFE STORE.

Hey, says the woman, you ever see one of those shows where the guy throws the knives at the lady?

Yeah, says her friend, and the lady doesn't get hurt?

Yeah! says the woman. We should do that!

Okay! says the friend. Okay, if you want!

So the two buy lots of knives and run off to go practice.

Do you want to throw or catch? the woman says a moment later.

Catch! says the friend. I mean . . . !

Both women laugh, and then the friend goes to the wall, and the woman tentatively takes aim.

Be careful! says the friend.

I will! says the woman.

And she rears back and starts to throw.

The knife flies cleanly through the air—and lands perfectly in the center of the friend's stomach.

In the hospital, the friend is very angry.

You're the one who wanted to catch, says the woman.

Yeah, says the friend, but not with my body!

I told you I was sorry, says the woman.

A few months later, the friend is released. She calls up the woman on the phone.

Are you ready? she says. 'Cuz this time it's my turn.

Ready, the woman's answer finally comes.

The two of them meet at the practicing spot. The woman brings the bucket of knives.

Here you go, she says, handing it to the friend. I'll go stand in front of the wall.

The friend assumes the thrower's position, and chooses a knife from the bucket.

This one looks sharp, she grins. Very sharp. Let's hope it doesn't hurt too much.

The friend squints her eyes and bends forward like a pitcher, then straightens up and goes into the windup. The knife hand comes up, and the knife hand goes back, and then the knife hand comes forward.

The blade flies out cleanly, whistling through the air, like an arrow toward the woman by the wall.

It's just about to plunge into her heart—
When abruptly, it disappears.

What? says the woman. Where did it go?
    I don't know! says the friend. And I almost had you!
    The two stand in silence, looking around.
    Do you think it'll come back? the woman says.

It sure doesn't look like it, the friend finally says.
    Well, says the woman. What do we do now? Do you
want to try a different knife?
    They look to the bucket.
    All of the knives are gone.

Hmm, says the friend. This is strange.
    Yes, says the woman. I agree. And also, on top of that,
I'm really getting tired of standing by the wall like this.
    Well, says the friend. Let's do something else.
    Like what? says the woman. A movie?
    I don't know, says the friend. Anything, really. This
whole knife thing got really boring.

So the two women link arms and slowly walk away, leaving the empty bucket behind.
    For a while, the world is silent and still.
    And then, off in the distance, there's laughing.

THE FISH IN THE TEAPOT

A MAN FINDS A FISH IN HIS TEAPOT.

Hmm, he says. That's odd.

He decides to transfer the fish to a bowl. He does, and watches it for a while.

It seems like a good fish, he says to himself. I just don't get how it got in the teapot.

The man tells his friend about the fish in the teapot.

Someone must be playing a joke on you, his friend says.

Who? says the man. And what kind of joke is that?

I don't know, says his friend. But what's the other explanation?

The man sits at home, watching the fish, trying to figure out what's happened.

Who put you in my teapot? he says to the fish.

But the fish doesn't bother to answer.

It just swims around the bowl looking for an exit.

That night the man has a dream. In his dream all his friends are leaving his house with teapots tucked under their arms. Apparently the man has hundreds of teapots—and also hundreds of friends—for the dream seems to go on for hours and hours.

Good lord, says the man, waking up.

He goes into the kitchen and stares at his teapot. Of course, there is only one.

I must be losing my mind, the man says.

Then he looks at the bowl.

The fish is gone.

What the hell? says the man.

He looks all around. He checks the counter, the floor, under the fridge. He goes into the dining room and searches there too. He checks the living room and the bedroom to be sure. Then he goes into the bathroom and checks the toilet and the tub.

But the fish is gone.

Completely gone.

It's gotta be one of my friends, the man says. Probably the same one who left the fish to begin with.

He hunts around and finds his address book, puts it in his pocket, and goes out.

The man goes to visit every friend he has. He pushes into their homes and stomps around. He interrogates them and the members of their families, and peers into their closets and drawers.

But he can find neither hide nor hair of his fish, and all of his friends are frowning.

You were never my friend to begin with, one says.

We don't like you, says another. Please leave.

When the man crosses off the last name in his book—still shy one particular fish—he finds a policeman waiting outside.

You'll have to come with me, sir, the policeman says.

The man is taken to jail and thrown in a cell.

All I wanted was my fish! he says.

What fish is that? says a prisoner beside him.

Oh, it doesn't matter, the man says.

He sits there and sits there for hours and hours.

He realizes it matters very much.

When the man is released, he hurries on home and immediately looks in the kitchen. The fish is still gone; the teapot's still there. He looks inside it to be sure, but there's nothing.

The man stands in the kitchen. He doesn't know what to do. He thinks about making some tea, but for some reason he just doesn't feel like it.

Perhaps I will buy a fish, he thinks.

The man goes down to the neighborhood pet store. Inside, he finds hundreds of fish. He walks up and down all the aisles.

My God, he thinks, there must be thousands.

He wanders the pet store for what seems like hours, staring and staring into the tanks. But none of the fish he sees seems right; none is the fish from his pot.

Finally the man decides to ask the lady sitting behind the counter.

In your teapot? she frowns. That's very strange. I don't know what kind of fish that would be. What kind of teapot do you have, exactly?

The man hems and haws. He makes a tentative motion with his hands.

It's hard to describe, he says.

The man and the woman go back to his house. They stand there in the kitchen, looking down.

Hmm, says the woman, I still don't know. It is a nice teapot, though.

The man and the woman sit at the table and drink tea from the man's best cups. The man tells the woman about the weird things that have happened, and the woman listens, and then tells him some back.

My cousin got his porch stolen one time, she says.

His whole porch? says the man, in wonder.

Yep, says the woman.

And they drink their tea.

Later, they go out for supper.

THE GIRL IN THE STORM

THERE ONCE WAS A GIRL WHO WAS LOST IN A STORM. She wandered this way and that, this way and that, trying to find a way home. But the sky was too dark, and the rain too fierce; all the girl did was go in circles.

Then, suddenly, there were arms around her. Strong arms—good strong arms. And they picked the girl up and carried her away.

When she woke, she was lying in bed.

It was a warm bed—very warm—by a roaring fire. The blankets were soft, and she was dry. She looked around the room. There were paintings on the walls.

There was a hot cup of tea on the nightstand.

Hello? called the girl. Hello? Hello?

A young man appeared in the doorway. He looked down at the girl with a kind, quiet smile.

Feel better? he said.

And she did.

The girl stayed with the man for quite a long time, until she had all her strength back.

I guess it's time for me to go home, she said, and started to gather her clothes.

But when she got to the door, she saw the rain was still falling. If anything, it was falling even harder. So she took off her clothes again, and went back to bed, and lay in the man's arms a little longer.

This went on for many, many years, and eventually the girl grew very old.

And then one day she discovered on the wall by the door the switch that turned the rain on and off.

She stood there staring at the beautiful day outside, and then down at the simple little switch. She listened as the birds flew by the window, singing.

And then she turned and went back to bed.

In the night, that night, the man woke up.

Did the rain stop? he said. I dreamt it did.

And the girl put her arms around the man and held him tight.

It may have, she said. But it's all right.

THE AFTERLIFE IS
WHAT YOU LEAVE BEHIND

A MAN STOCKPILES BELONGINGS FOR THE NEXT LIFE. HE buys coats, jackets, hats, socks, shoes; he buys umbrellas and belts and pretty flowers and couches and sports cars and big urns made of gold. He lines his house with hundreds of boxes of coins, bullion, stamps, paper banknotes. The man buys everything he thinks could be of use; the man buys everything he can.

Then one day the man becomes ill—deathly ill.
    Here it comes, he says.
    And he readies his belongings and lies down to die.
    I sure hope this works, he says.

But as he's lying there, a woman comes to him.
    Come with me awhile, she says.

And the man gets up, and quietly goes with her, and is never seen or heard from again.

In the morning, the man's nurse arrives early, only to find her employer mysteriously gone. A funeral follows after some time, but as the man had no friends, they don't come.

But that night, as the man's house stands empty, a breeze cracks a window and slips in. It glides over the couches, the jackets, the gold, smells the flowers, and tries on the shoes.

And then it laughs, the breeze, and it smiles a little, and it whirls once more about the room. And then it flits back out the open window and is gone, with no plans to come again soon.

THE TREE

A TREE STANDS IN THE FOREST. IT STANDS THERE FOR many years—watching animals go by, watching people go by, watching birds go by, watching clouds go by. It stands there, and it stands there, and it stands there, and it stands there.

And then one day it decides to move.

I'm going to walk, says the tree, and it does.

It lifts its roots up out of the ground. And then it shakes them off, one by one, and heads off across the countryside.

At first, the going is rather hard, but then the tree gets the hang of it.

What are you doing? the other trees say.

I'm going to see the world, says the tree.

The tree walks and walks for miles and miles. It sees many interesting things—a well, a bucket, an old barn, a rusted sign.

It finds a road, and follows it a great distance.

Finally the tree comes up over a hill and sees a town spread out before it.

A town! thinks the tree. This must be a town!

And it hurries down the road toward the buildings.

When it gets to the town, the people come out to greet it.

A walking tree! they all say. A walking tree!

Everyone seems so excited to see it; the tree is very, very happy.

Hello everybody! the tree says, and waves its limbs around.

The people laugh and dance with it.

Let's have a celebration! they say.

So the tree goes with the people down to the park that lies in the center of town, and everyone laughs and dances and sings, and tells stories deep into the night.

But when the tree awakens in the morning, it finds itself alone. And surrounding it is a tall iron fence.

What is this? says the tree.

It cranes over the top to get a better look. There is something on the front of the fence. The something is a metal block-lettered sign.

THE WALKING TREE, it says.

The tree paces back and forth in the enclosure. It tries the iron fence, but it's too strong.

How did this happen? the tree says aloud.

But there is no response.

The tree doesn't know what to do. Every day people come and stare at it. It talks to them, asks them why it's been imprisoned, but no one pays any attention.

Look, all the people tell their children, look, it's the walking tree.

And everyone acts like the tree's not even there—except as something to see.

Finally, the tree just gives up. It goes to the center of the enclosure. It slides its roots down into the ground, and then it closes its eyes.

And it sleeps, and it sleeps, and it sleeps, and it sleeps.

And then it sleeps some more.

The years go by. The fence starts to rust. Fewer people come by to see the tree.

It's not walking, all the children say.
It doesn't do it very often, say the parents.

Eventually, the people in the town forget that the tree ever even *could* walk.

"The Walking Tree" is just a name, they say. That's just what they call it.

And finally, the people in the town stop coming to see the tree at all. It just sits there quietly by itself, surrounded by the tall iron fence. Even the sign that used to hang there that said THE WALKING TREE is gone. It rusted away and fell to the ground, and was buried and has been long forgotten.

And then, after many, many years, the mayor of the town makes a decision.

That rusted old fence should be taken down, he says. It's unsightly, and there for no reason.

And so the fence is taken down, and dragged away and destroyed, and only the tree stands in the park.

And now the tree opens its eyes.

Ah, says the tree, now's my chance!

And it goes to take its roots out of the ground.

But when it does, it suddenly finds it can't move them—can't budge them at all.

What? says the tree, and pulls and pulls. But its roots won't move an inch.

They've grown so deep, they're sunk in fast.

The tree frowns and looks around.

And that's when the tree suddenly sees that the town is completely gone. In fact, the land itself is gone!

And then the tree looks down.

There below—way, way, way below—the tree can see the town. It's so far below, it's just a spot.

The tree, you see, has grown.

The tree has matured and become muscular and strong. Its bark is thick and healthy. Its leaves are many, wide, and green; it towers high into the sky.

The tree has become magnificent. Straight and proud and tall.

And now it can't even see the town—that spot might have been a rock, after all.

Off to the side, the tree sees a river, and beside that a little hill. And behind that, a group of little mountains; a little vale, a little dell.

And beyond that, the tree can see the coast, and beyond *that* the ocean wide. And scattered throughout, a million islands, and more land on the other side.

The tree can see the whole wide world; every inch, every mile. The tree looks around; it stretches out.

Hello, say the passing clouds.

The tree smiles back, and then looks up, and overhead, it sees the sun. And it reaches up and touches it.

While below, little people run.

THE SEA MONSTER

THE MEN OF THE ISLAND ARE OUT HUNTING SEA MON-sters when one of them falls overboard. The others search for him all night long, but there is no trace, no sign of him, nothing.

Eventually, in the morning, they give up and head home.

Sorrow hangs over them as they row.

Upon arrival, however, the men are surprised to find their vanished comrade walking the streets of the town. When questioned, he claims to have never gone on the expedition.

I felt sick, he says, so I stayed home.

The men of the town can only stare at him. They were there, with him, on the boat. They saw him fall into the cold, dark water. They heard him cry as he fell.

They watch him now as he tells his story. He tells it

again and again. Yet no matter how many times the men hear it, they know that it cannot be true.

But then—on the other hand—this they also know: the man could not have swum home. Not from that distance, not at night, not in waters that cold.

It simply could not have happened.

Either way.

Either way, it just isn't possible.

And so, in the end, there is nothing to do. One by one, the men return to their homes. They try to turn their backs on the mystery the man presents, and go back to the world that makes sense.

But from that day on, no one trusts the man. The eyes of the town turn upon him. He can't go anywhere without knowing he's being watched, can't say anything without feeling he's doubted.

And, in time, the man rebels.

In time, the man becomes angry.

I just didn't want to go on that ridiculous hunt! he says. Why is that so hard to understand?

The man begins to drink, then drinks more and more. One night in a tavern there's a fight. Two men have been staring at him for too long.

One of them pulls a knife.

The man is found guilty of first-degree murder and is quickly sentenced to be hanged.

I acted in self-defense, he says. You all know I'm a peaceful man!

But no one in the courtroom even looks at him; no one cares what he says. The jury files out through the back door. The judge turns away from the bench.

The sentence is carried out in the town square, one year to the day after the hunt.

The entire town stands in attendance.

The hanging does not go well.

The man's neck does not snap when the platform drops. Instead, he writhes at the end of the rope until suffocation finally takes him.

The people of the town watch it all.

They stand there silently and do not turn away until the man's lifeless body comes to rest.

Well, that's that, they say to one another. Guess that puts an end to that.

But that night, the people do not sleep well. They do not sleep well at all. In their minds, they see the sea—the cold, dark sea—and in the sea, they see monsters. The monsters are rising; they are coming forth. They are climbing, crawling, sliding up the sand. They are moving over the island, toward the town, moving through the streets of the town. They are moving around and under and over and through all the houses of the town, licking and smelling and touching and feeling and tasting the sleeping people of the town. They are laughing their hard, shrill sea monster laughs, and waving their prehensile hooked limbs.

And then all the monsters are in the town square, and they are raising up the hanged man.

In the morning, the townspeople rise as one and walk to the square and stand looking.

There, from the gallows, a body is still hanging.

But the body is not that of the man.

By the stroke of noon, the ships are embarking. The bowsprits point the way. The nets have been patched, and the harpoons are sharpened.

This time, the men are shackled in place.

THE MAN AND THE MOOSE

A MOOSE IS STANDING IN THE FOREST WHEN HE SUDdenly hears a noise. He looks up and sees a plane flying overhead. As he watches, a man jumps out. A parachute bursts open and the man floats safely down.

The moose goes over and looks at him.

Hello, says the man, gathering in his parachute.

Hello, says the moose. What are you doing?

Oh nothing, says the man. Nothing much. I just jump out of planes every now and then.

The moose looks up at the sky.

Is it fun? he says.

Oh yes, says the man. Have you never done it?

Me? says the moose. Oh, no.

Well come along with me, says the man. We'll go back to town and get you all suited up, and then off we'll go. What do you say?

I don't know, says the moose. Isn't it dangerous?

Dangerous? says the man. No, not at all! Well, a little, but hey, isn't everything?

I guess, says the moose. When you put it that way.

And after a while, he starts to nod.

All right, he says. Okay.

Great! says the man. You're gonna love it!

And he claps the moose on the back and the two of them start off.

When they get to the edge of the city, the moose suddenly stops.

What about the people? he says.

What about 'em? says the man.

Well, says the moose, I'm not saying that I'm afraid of them, understand. But they're always out in the woods *looking* at me. It makes me nervous. I don't know what they want.

Hmm, says the man. I doubt they want anything. But okay, here's what we'll do.

He takes an extra T-shirt and a hat out of his bag.

Put these on, nobody'll recognize you, he says.

The moose looks at the offered disguise for a moment.

All right, he says, and puts it on.

The man and the moose wander into town. The moose is very, very nervous.

Hey Tom! someone says, and a group of people come over. How'd your jump go today? And who's that?

The man turns and looks at the moose.

This is my friend Lawrence, he says. He just came in from the coast.

The moose shakes hands all around.

Quite a grip you got there, Lawrence, says one of the men.

Are you bringing Lawrence to the party? says another.

Shoot, says the man, looking at the moose, I completely forgot about that. You mind coming along to this thing tonight? It's sort of a shindig for my most recent jump.

Sure, says the moose, feeling self-conscious. Sure, that'll be fine.

That night the man and the moose go to the party. It is at The Explorers Club. There are a number of long tables arranged in a square. The man and the moose are in the place of honor.

The moose is having a wonderful time. The food is really very good. Different people make different speeches, and the moose finds the waitress quite fascinating.

But then, suddenly, something draws his attention: heads—animal heads. They're lining the walls, all around the top. Lions, zebras, deer, elk . . . and moose.

Fear grips the moose's heart.

Killers, he thinks, looking around the room.

What is it? says the man, sensing trouble.

The moose turns and looks at him in horror.

You're trying to kill me, he says, his voice a whisper. You brought me here to kill me!

What? says the man. Why would I do that? I don't understand.

But the moose is too scared to explain. He stumbles backward to his feet. He points a hoof at the abomination on the wall.

The man sees it. Then his eyes go wide.

My God! he says. I just didn't think!

He reaches out to reassure the moose.

But his hand grabs the T-shirt and it rips and falls off, and then, to make matters worse, the moose's hat tumbles to the floor.

Everybody turns.

A moose! they cry. Get him! Get him! Get the guns!

The moose takes off. He galumphs out of the ballroom, knocking people over left and right. He barrels through the doors and off down the hall.

The members of The Explorers Club are striking the glass on the gun cases.

Hurry! they are yelling. It's a big one! The biggest!

The moose careens out into the street. He's weaving in and out of cars. There's honking and screaming. The moose has never been so terrified.

Wait! Wait! cries a voice.

The moose looks back. It's the man, running after him.

I'm sorry, yells the man. I didn't think! I'm so stupid! I'll make it up to you! I'll get you out of this! I swear!

Are you kidding? yells the moose. Why should I trust you?

Just then, gunfire erupts. It's The Explorers Club, hot on their trail. Bullets whiz past—close, closer.

I can take you to the plane! says the man. It's your only chance!

The moose thinks.

Another bullet whizzes by.

All right, the moose yells, climb on!

The man jumps on and the two of them charge through the streets.

Turn left! yells the man, and the moose turns.

Up ahead is the airfield. Behind, the men with guns—getting closer with every passing second.

There's the plane! the man hollers, and the two dive on board. The man guns it and the plane taxis toward the runway.

Behind them, The Explorers Club lines up in a row.

Fire! says the leader. Fire more!

The plane is hit in ten thousand places, but still it manages to lift off. Behind, it trails a cloud of smoke and fire that is terrifying to behold.

We're not going to make it! the man yells to the moose. We're going to have to jump!

He turns and looks for the parachutes, but there is only one.

You take it, says the man, pushing it to the moose.

But the moose just stares at it in silence.

No, you, says the moose. I don't even know how to use it. Besides, I wouldn't have gotten this far without you.

The man thinks for a moment.

We go together, he finally says. It might work, it might not, who knows.

He straps the parachute around them both and edges the moose toward the door.

On the count of three, the man says.

And the moose jumps.

The man and the moose plummet through the air.

Is that the forest? the moose calls. Down there?

Yes! says the man. Isn't it pretty?

It is! says the moose. I can see why you like doing this!

At this point, the ground is coming up pretty fast.

All right, says the man. Moment of truth!

The two grip the pull-cord tightly together.

I hope we can be friends, says the moose.

THE END OF IT ALL

A MAN AND A WOMAN FALL IN LOVE AND ARE MARRIED, and are happy in every single way.

Then one day a flying saucer lands in their backyard, and a door opens, and an alien comes out.

I'm going to have to take one of you away, it says.

What? say the man and woman. Why?

I don't know, says the alien. That's just how it is.

And in the end, the woman gets taken away.

The man, of course, is extremely upset. He goes to the United Nations.

An alien stole my wife! he says. You have to do something!

We're sorry, says the UN, we don't deal with aliens.

The man goes to see the folks over at NASA.

We can barely get to the moon, NASA says. You'd be better off trying to build a ship on your own.

Okay, says the man.

He goes to the bookstore.

The man has never really been to the bookstore. He finds lots of interesting books there: science, and technology, computers, and how to build things.

He buys them all and goes home and reads.

After some time, the man thinks he's ready. He builds a spaceship in his backyard. The first one doesn't start, and the second one explodes, but the third one runs perfectly, like a dream.

So the man throws a whole bunch of food in a bag, picks up a gallon jug of water, grabs the photo of his wife off the piano, and gets in, turns the key, and takes off.

The man looks for years. He flies all around space, from one end to another and then back. He discovers many planets, many galaxies and stars. He even discovers a wide assortment of alien civilizations.

But every time the man asks: Have you seen this woman? all eyes stare blankly at the photograph.

No, they all say. We haven't seen that woman. And what's more, we've never seen a photograph.

Finally, after many, many, many years of searching, the man returns to Earth in defeat. He has become old—and very sad.

The UN welcomes him with a grand ceremony.

For introducing our world to the great family of the stars, the secretary-general says, we give you this medal. And also this certificate. We hope you will hang it on the wall.

The newspapers are full of accounts of the man's exploits. Biographies are written, portraits painted. Somebody somewhere composes a cantata. Streets are built and called the man's name.

But the man doesn't care about any of that. He sits in his house and thinks of his wife. He remembers every single detail about her: what she looked like, where they met, what she liked and thought and said.

He remembers it all, just like it was yesterday.

He remembers it all, every day.

And then, finally, on his dying day, the man gets up and goes into the yard. He stands gazing up into the sky. Overhead, the stars twinkle down.

It was worth it! the man cries. It was worth it just to know you! It was worth it just to even know your name!

And in response, the sky explodes.

The gates of heaven open in flame.

ON THE WAY DOWN:

A STORY FOR RAY BRADBURY

A MAN JUMPS OFF A CLIFF.

I'm gonna need some wings, he thinks.

He reaches into his backpack to get some things—wood, nails, a hammer, some string—and then gets down to work building.

That ground is coming up awful fast, he thinks. I'd better work a little quicker.

The wings he's building just begin to flap—

When the man suddenly slams into the ground.

Little bits of the man go everywhere.

It's a mess.

Really, it's awful.

But then, lo! The angel rises up—effortlessly, out of the wreckage.

You know, it says, these actually work quite well!

And it whizzes off to find breakfast.

THE HOUSE ON THE
CLIFF AND THE SEA

THE SEA WAS ROLLING ALONG ONE DAY, JUST AS IT always did, when it looked up and saw a little house perched on top of a cliff.

What a beautiful house! the sea said. It just looks so inviting!

And then it saw that the house was smiling down at it, and waving.

Oh sea! called the house. I've watched you so long, and always admired you so. Why don't you come up and stay for a while? Isn't it time you found a home?

Oh, yes! cried the sea. Oh, yes, it is! And I'd love to come stay with you!

So it reached for the cliff, and took hold with its waves, and started to climb the rock face.

But as the sea found, its waves weren't suited to grasping and holding things, and as a result it had a hard time even starting to climb such a cliff. And—what's more—every time it *did* make progress, gravity would reach right up, and grab the sea with its heavy hands, and dash it down on the rocks.

But the sea was determined. It would not give up. It started to climb again and again. It tried and tried with everything it had to make its way to the house. It climbed with every ounce of its being; it fell without giving a damn. It got back up again and again.

The sea would not stay down.

And meanwhile, up on top of the cliff, the house busied itself preparing. It cleaned and scrubbed and put itself in order and swept out all of the dust. It set the table with its very best china, and baked pies and breads and muffins and cakes and scones. And it made very sure that the hedges were cut, and there were notepads and pens by the phone.

And when the house was all set—and this took a long time—it went to see how the sea was progressing. But when it looked down, it saw the sea at the bottom.

Still at the bottom—but still trying.

I'm sorry, the sea said, looking up at the house, but I just can't seem to do it. I try and I try, but the fact of it is, I just don't have the strength to climb this cliff.

Well, that's okay! the house said, looking down. Don't be silly—don't worry so much! If you can't come up here, I'll just go down there. This is no problem we can't overcome!

Really? said the sea.

Really! said the house.

And it got ready to make the big leap. But when it did, something very strange happened—

The house didn't go anyplace.

What the . . . ? said the house, looking around. How odd—I seem to be tied down!

Tied down? said the sea.

Yes, said the house. There's this thing I think they call a foundation? And then there are all of these weird pipes, and spaghetti-like strands of buzzing metal. They're everywhere—everywhere!—wrapped all around me! How did these things get here?

What if you just pull really hard? said the sea, from its place at the bottom of the cliff.

So the house pulled and pulled and pulled and pulled, but it was just no use.

Oh sea, cried the house, I don't know what to do! I'm trapped here; I'm stuck here for good! It doesn't matter how hard I try, these things just won't let me go!

The sea didn't know what to do or say—and there was really nothing it *could* do. The house was trapped at the top of the cliff, and the sea was a million miles away.

I'll just stay down here, the sea finally said. We can tell each other stories.

Really? said the house. That would be nice.

And so that's what they did.

They told each other all about themselves, about

everything they'd ever seen or done. The sea talked about the origins of life, and the house described its living room.

And as the years passed, the two grew very close, even though of course the cliff was between them.

And then one day—out of the blue—the cliff just crumbled away.

Who knows, it may have just been an accident—maybe an earthquake down below. Or maybe the sea's attempts to climb the cliff had worn the rock away. Or maybe the house's tug-of-war with its foundation had somehow started the process. Or maybe—just maybe—it was all the talking. Maybe it tired the cliff out.

Or maybe it was none of that—or all that—or more. But whatever it was, the cliff crumbled. And, as it did—as it fell through the air—so too fell the little house.

Aaa! cried the house. I'm falling! I'm falling!

It's okay, said the sea. I've got you.

And it reached up and caught the house with its waves, and set it down in the shallows.

And now, today, the two are together. They wander the world as one. They eat cakes and scones and lots of fish, and every now and then some coconuts.

The sea doesn't care much for the land anymore, but sometimes they drift on by. And the house smiles and waves at its friends on the shore, and then they drift on some more.

At night, the sea lies there and listens to the house creaking gently as it floats, and tries to remember that it now has a new name.

A house on the sea is a boat.

THE SNAKE IN THE THROAT

A MAN FINDS SOMETHING IN HIS THROAT. HE REACHES
in and pulls it out.

It's a snake.

What are you doing in my throat? the man says.

Nothing, says the snake. Just hanging out.

The man stares at it.

There's something you're not telling me, isn't there?
he says.

But all the snake does is look away.

The man puts the snake in a jar and closes the lid. He
sits around and stares at it all day.

What are you doing? his friends say.

I found this in my throat, says the man.

The man's friends stare at the snake.

That's disgusting, they say. Why don't you kill it?

Kill it? says the man.

He looks at the snake.

I hadn't really thought of that, he says.

Long after his friends have left, the man sits with the snake. He imagines himself bashing it with a rock.

Don't do it, says the snake. It would be a mistake.

Really? says the man. In what way?

You would regret it, says the snake. You would feel bad.

Can't you just tell me why you were in there? says the man. Can't you just tell me what you were up to?

But the snake just shakes its head.

I wasn't up to anything, it says. I already told you. See, that's your problem—you're distrustful.

The man takes the snake out back and finds a big rock.

Last chance, he says. Last chance.

Go ahead, says the snake, staring right back up at him. Do it if you think it'll help.

The man brings the rock down on the snake's head. He brings it down again and again. He grinds the snake's head into a sickening pulp. Then he throws the body away.

Later that evening, the man goes out with his friends.

How's that snake? they say. Still in the jar?

I killed it, says the man.

His friends stop and stare.

I killed it with a rock, says the man.

The rest of the evening is rather subdued.

I have to go, says one of the man's friends.

My wife is expecting me, says another one.

Yeah, says a third. See you next time.

Finally, it is just the man, sitting alone at the table. He sits alone for quite some time. Drinking, and thinking, and thinking.

Outside the door he finds a rock.

The man goes to the house of one of his friends, and smashes his head with the rock. Then he goes to the house of another of his friends, and does the same thing to him. He smashes the heads of all of his friends, and then he walks away. He walks to a field on the edge of town and lies down on his belly to pray.

Please God, says the man, out loud to himself. Please God, I'm sorry I did that. I had no idea I could do such a thing. I didn't even know I had it in me.

THE GRAVEYARD

A MAN MOVES INTO A GRAVEYARD. IT IS VERY NICE—very quiet. He sets up a tent under a tree. He has a small collection of canned goods, which he cooks in a skillet over a portable burner. He plays the harmonica sometimes, and has a phone book he reads when he's bored.

Isn't it creepy out there? people say.

Creepy? says the man. No, not at all. In fact, it's really quite pleasant.

But then one night the man awakens to find cold, dead hands trying to drag him underground.

Aah! shrieks the man. He bashes the hands with the skillet. Let go! Let go! Let go!

The hands release him and retreat into the earth, but the man can't get back to sleep that night.

I wonder what they want from me? the man thinks. I wonder what's down there in the ground?

You have to move, everyone says. That's ridiculous.

No, says the man. It's okay. I figured it out. I just buy some steel sheets and lay them on the ground. Then I sleep on those. The hands won't be able to get through the steel, and I'll be safe!

And he does it, and sleeps soundly for the next three nights or four.

But on the fifth night the man is awakened again. A group of six cadavers have lifted him up from his bed on the steel sheet, and are carrying him toward a large hole in the ground nearby.

No! says the man. No! I don't want to go!

The man kicks and fights. The idea of going down into the ground sickens him. He fights like a wild animal. And—perhaps because the corpses are dead, and poorly coordinated—he escapes.

He runs from the graveyard in terror.

Are you done now? say the people. Ready to live some-place normal?

But the man looks down at his feet.

It's so nice in the graveyard, he says. It's relaxing. Really, it is!

The people throw their hands in the air.

The man goes back, but takes to sleeping during the day.

They don't come out then, he says.

And all night long—every night—he sits there, with his skillet clutched in one hand. Playing the harmonica and reading the phone book, and fighting the cadavers when they come.

It's not a bad existence, he says to himself. I mean, it's sad not seeing the sun; the graveyard is so pretty in the daytime. But it's also nice at night—and quieter.

Well, he amends, except when they come, and I have to fight for my life.

The weeks and months and years go by, and the man has it down to a science. He's no longer even really scared of the cadavers. In fact, he's just bored by the whole thing.

I don't even know what's down there, he starts to wonder. All this effort to stay out, and I have no idea. Plus I'm tired of this same old rectangular graveyard. I need a change of scenery. Something.

A few times he decides to leave and go out for a walk, but for some reason now the gates are always locked.

So finally, one final night, when the cadavers come, the man stands and goes peacefully with them. And the dead men lead him down into the dark, dark earth, into a grotto lit by phosphorescent lichen.

The man looks around and sees he is surrounded— by hundreds, thousands of cadavers. All of them lying out on blankets on their backs, underneath the rocky, "starry" sky.

Somewhere in the distance, a harmonica is playing a quiet, plaintive song. And all around, the cadavers are turning the pages of their phone books, and reading on and on.

So this is what you do down here? the man finally says. Just lie around and read?

But nobody answers; no one says a word.

I'll go get my book too, the man says.

The man lives underground with the dead men for some time. He can't believe how much reading he gets done. But finally, one day, he reaches the end of his book.

Well, he says, I guess I'll make some calls.

The man climbs slowly back to the surface, brushes himself off, and heads for the gate. The combination on the lock stops him for a while, but trial and error eventually take the day.

He stumbles into town and finds a phone booth. He starts right in with the *A*'s.

Party at my place! he says to everyone. Come one, come all! he says.

Nobody wants to come, but he just keeps dialing.
Bring a friend! he says. Bring everyone!
But not a single person in the world is interested.
No one, not even Mr. Zzzz.

Still, the man is not disheartened.

They'll change their minds, he thinks.

So he buys a nice bean dip and heads back home, picks up his harmonica, and waits.

THE FERRIS WHEEL

A BOY AND A GIRL GO DOWN TO THE PIER AND TAKE A ride on the Ferris wheel. When they get to the top, the gondola stops. They look out.

It's beautiful, says the girl.

It is, says the boy, and then he smiles. We should get married up here!

Oh! says the girl. What a wonderful idea!

The only question is when, says the boy.

What? says the girl, and she looks at him, and then she looks away.

What is it? says the boy.

Nothing, says the girl.

And the wheel takes them back down to the bottom.

But when they're out in the crowd, the boy suddenly realizes the girl is no longer there. He turns to look around—he looks all around—but he can't see any sign of her anywhere. He searches the pier all night long, but all he finds are strangers around him. And when the night is over, the boy is kicked out, and has to go home, alone.

The boy spends the next day looking for the girl. But she isn't at her home or her work. He alerts the authorities and searches for weeks, but nothing ever seems to come of it.

Time goes by, and the years stretch out, and still the boy wonders what happened. Where did she go? Where is she now? And does she ever think about him?

But there's no way to know, and the boy grows old, and his life is empty and sad.

And then one day he knows he's going to die.

I still don't know what happened, he says.

The boy (now an old man) goes down to the pier. It takes him a while, but he gets there. He stands staring up at the old Ferris wheel, remembering the time he spent there with the girl.

Would you like to get on? the operator says, and the old man nods his head. And he gets in the gondola and goes for a ride, and at the top he finds the girl waiting there.

She's sitting in the gondola, right beside him, and her hair is drifting in the breeze. And she looks at him, and she's smiling and waving.

You finally came back, she says.

And the boy looks at her, and he takes her hand, and he gets down on one knee.

Marry me, he says. Marry me right now.

But we've been married this whole time, she says.

And then the boy sees that she's an old woman, just as he's an old man. And the two of them are wearing their wedding rings, just as they always have been.

Oh, says the old man, I must have dozed off.

It's okay, says the woman, it's late.

And the two of them kiss and pull up the blankets, and hold each other through the night.

PHOTOGRAPHS

THE MAN HAS A PROBLEM. HIS FOOT DOESN'T LOOK right. He can't tell exactly in what way. It's just different, somehow; there's something wrong with it. He keeps eyeing it, trying to figure it out.

He starts sorting through old photos of himself, looking for a good one of his foot. With a photo, he'd be able to tell instantly. But the only ones he can find are blurry and indistinct.

All these years and not a single good close-up of my foot, says the man. This is terrible.

He looks down again at his problematic foot.

I really need to be more careful, he says.

A moment later, the man starts taking pictures.

He takes pictures of every part of his body. Arms, legs, fingers, toes, knees, eyebrows, elbows. He takes very good, clean close-ups. Well lit. From dozens of angles.

Then he puts the photographs up on the wall.

That oughtta do it, he says.

Now every day when the man gets up, he goes immediately to the wall. He checks what he sees there against his actual body, to make sure everything is still the same.

It seems to be a pretty good system.

I think we've got this under control, he says.

Then one morning the man wakes up, only to find that all the photographs have changed.

The man stares at the photos in shocked disbelief.

What the . . . ? he says. What on earth?

Very carefully, he tries to match the strange body parts in the photos to the parts of his actual body.

And that's when he notices that the parts of his body have all suddenly changed as well.

My God, the man thinks, and runs into the bathroom. He stands there, staring into the mirror.

The man in the mirror is completely different.

The man is no longer himself.

What's going on here? the man cries out loud.

He runs his hands through his hair.

It's me, right? he says. It's me! I'm me? It's me?

He looks, but the man in the mirror doesn't answer.

Okay, says the man, think, think, think, staring at the strange face in the mirror. The photos are wrong but I'm wrong too—but I'm me inside—have I gone insane?

Then, a moment later, he's suddenly figured it out.

It's the pictures! he says. The pictures did this!

He runs into the other room and tears them from the wall, grabs the lighter fluid, and heads into the yard.

He stands and watches as the photos burn and the smoke drifts up into the sky.

Thank God that's over, the man says after a while. That one was way too close.

Then the man remembers the horrible face that the mirror in the bathroom showed him.

Oh God, he says. I can't go back in there. What if that face is still there?

So he picks up a crowbar, puts a hand over his eyes, and goes in and smashes the mirror to pieces.

All right, he says. That settles that. Finally, that chapter's closed.

But is the chapter closed? No. No, it's not.

Now the man has a bathroom with a gaping hole where the mirror was, and a wall in the living room that reminds him of the photographs.

Now all the man thinks about is what isn't there.

Now all he does is lie in bed.

One day the man awakens in the hospital.

Do you feel okay? says the nurse.

I don't know, says the man. Am I really sick?

Well, says the nurse, could be worse.

The man sells his house and moves to another state. A warm state, a state with a coastline. He buys a house that's on the beach and makes juice every morning from fruit that grows on a tree in his yard.

The man even has a mirror in his house. He looks into it from time to time. He was nervous at first, but it's all right now—as long as he doesn't stare very long.

The man spends a lot of time wandering around. He plays shuffleboard and makes some new friends. The more of them he meets, the more he learns that there are other stories like his.

Yeah, says one fellow. The photos got me too. Shoulda never messed with the things.

Me too, says a woman, shaking her head. I thought it would be a good idea, but it wasn't.

It really wasn't, she adds, looking over at the man. Really, you know, it wasn't.

The man lies in bed at night thinking it over. None of it makes any sense.

The whole thing's terrifying, he says, and then looks down. On the other hand, my foot's okay today.

So he gets out of bed and goes down to the beach, and stands there in his tattered robe. Overhead, a full moon shines down; below, sand nestles between his toes. The man stands and watches the waves for a while, and breathes in the cool night air. And then for a moment he closes his eyes.

And smiles.

The world is still there.

THE WALK THAT REPLACED
UNDERSTANDING

THE MAN DOESN'T KNOW WHAT'S HAPPENING. HE TRIES to understand, but he can't.

Eventually, he gives up.

I will go for a walk instead, he says.

The man walks out the door and is eaten by a lion.

Ouch, he says, and gets up and walks on.

He goes down to the store and buys a watermelon. He eats it all in one bite.

Sure is nice weather we're having, he says.

Then he sees the mountain approaching.

Hello, the man says to the mountain.

But the mountain just ignores him and walks by.

I wonder where the mountain is going? says the man.

And so he decides to follow it.

The man follows the mountain for miles and miles. It's hard to keep up; the mountain moves fast.

This would be so much easier if I was on top of the mountain, the man says.

So he runs really fast and jumps onto the mountain and climbs up onto its peak.

All around the man, the world moves past. Houses and sharks and trailer parks, and graffiti and Chinese restaurants. Envelopes and mossy rocks and oak trees and bars, and rainstorms and everything in between. Everything the man has ever seen or heard of or dreamt of, or *not* dreamt of—never dreamt of once—never dreamt of even one time.

It is really quite something, this parade of everything.

The man can't wait to see the rest of it.

Just then the mountain comes to the ocean. It starts to wade out and in.

Oh no, the man thinks. What do I do now?

The mountain is rapidly vanishing beneath the waves.

If I hang on, I'll drown, the man thinks. But I've become so attached to the view.

So in the end, he clings tightly with both hands to the peak as the mountain goes below.

With his eyes open, the man can see a large number of fish. There are bank fish and umbrella fish and refrigerator fish and math fish. There are dirt fish and chair fish and hate fish and car fish. There are some fish that the man doesn't know what kind of fish they are—and some fish where the man isn't even sure if they are fish!

Wow, the man says, this is really something!

But when he says that—when he opens his mouth—all the water rushes in.

And very quickly the man begins to drown.

Glug! says the man. Glug! Glug! Glug!

And he immediately lets go of the mountain.

The man is borne back up to the surface. He lies on the beach for a while. He vomits up an extremely large amount of saltwater—and a watermelon—and watches the sunset.

When night falls, the man decides it's time to go home. He stands up and brushes himself off.

All right, he says, now which way do I go?

He doesn't know; but luckily there are stars.

THE WOMAN AND THE BASEMENT

THE WOMAN HAS NEVER BEEN TO FRANCE BEFORE, AND neither does she want to go now. Same goes for England, Scotland, Egypt, Russia, Africa, Japan. The only place the woman wants to go is down into the basement. That's the only place she's interested in. And so that's where she's headed.

The woman packs a little picnic basket. She brings sandwiches and cookies and a thermos full of coffee. She also brings a flashlight; she figures she may need it.

At the last moment, she drinks a glass of water.

She's not sure how long she'll be gone.

The woman opens the door to the basement. There is a light switch; she flicks it on. The stairs are wood and make a pleasant sound—clop, clop, clop—as she goes down.

When she gets to the bottom, the woman looks around.

So this is the basement, she says.

It doesn't look like much—a big room, some shelves, a few cardboard boxes.

The woman walks around a little bit.

This is much smaller than I imagined, she says.

Then she notices the hidden door.

Oh, she says, and opens it.

The woman wanders down the passageway.

This is more like it, she says.

The passageway is narrow and very dark. The woman turns on the flashlight.

There are spiderwebs all over the place, and it is eerily quiet. The woman's heels make a clicking sound.

I wonder where this goes, she says.

Just then the passageway takes another turn.

Oh, says the woman, stopping short.

In front of her is a wall.

The passageway has come to an end.

The woman turns and looks around.

Maybe I missed a turnoff, she says.

She heads back the way she came. After a while she starts to frown.

Is this where I was before? she thinks. This doesn't look the same as it did.

She wanders and wanders and wanders and wanders.
She doesn't seem to get anyplace.

By now the woman is very hungry.

I guess it is lunchtime, she says.

She spreads a napkin on the floor, sits down, and opens the basket. She takes out a sandwich and then the cookies and the little thermos of coffee.

Mmm, she says. This coffee is good.

Just then the flashlight starts to die.

Oh, says the woman, taking another bite of her sandwich. I knew I should have brought extra batteries.

She eats the rest of her meal in the dark.

Well, she says, time to move on.

She puts the remains of her lunch in the basket—the thermos, the napkin, etc.—and then she stands and picks a direction.

Eenie meenie miney moe, she says.

The woman wanders along in the dark.

This sure is exciting, she says.

Every now and then she bumps into a wall.

Woops, she says. Guess it's not that way.

Finally, after many hours of wandering, the woman comes to a door.

Ah, she says, and opens it up.

Oh God, she says, and slams it closed.

The woman stands there in the dark. She doesn't know what to do. She takes a step back, but—as always—she's up against a wall. Same with the sides—both sides, just walls. It's the door, or nothing at all.

Fine, the woman thinks, let it be nothing.

And she stands there in the dark.

After a while, the woman grows tired, and finally she closes her eyes.

I'll just take a nap, she says to herself, and leans her head against the wall.

But when she opens her eyes again, she finds she's lying in bed.

Not her bed, but someone else's.

Why does this always happen? she says.

Outside the window, it is a beautiful day. She can see all the buildings standing there. So many of them, so clean, so bright, rising up into the air.

The woman sits and puts her feet on the floor. She

tries to find the strength to stand. She takes another look out the window.

Like it's hard to build *up*, she says.

In the kitchen, the woman finds the fridge is full, and there's a kettle of water on the stove.

When the kettle whistles, the woman picks it up.

In the cabinet will be a thermos.

The woman knows.

HADLEY

THE GUARD IS TAKING A HEAD COUNT, AND HE COMES UP one man short.

Hadley? the guard says. Hadley?

But Hadley isn't there.

What are we going to do? the guard says to the other guard.

I don't know, the other guard says. The warden is going to be mad.

The guard makes a big doll. The same size and shape as Hadley. He puts the doll in Hadley's cell.

That oughtta do it, says the other guard.

The days go by. Everything is fine. Mealtimes are the hardest part. The guard takes "Hadley" to the mess hall in chains, as though the prisoner were under close watch. He even cuts up Hadley's food and feeds it to him very carefully. Hadley is too dangerous, he insinuates, to be allowed to handle silverware.

The other prisoners all are fooled.

I wonder what Hadley did? they say.

They hope they don't do the same thing one day. Being fed by a guard would be humiliating.

Then one day something awful happens.

What is it? the guard says to the other guard.

The other guard is white as a sheet.

It's the warden, he says. He wants to see Hadley.

The guard escorts Hadley into the warden's office. He puts him in a chair and stands beside him.

You can go, the warden says. This is a private matter, just between Hadley and me.

The guard looks at the warden. Then he looks at Hadley.

I think he wants me to stay, he says.

The guard and the warden both look at Hadley.

Hadley doesn't reply.

The guard stands in the hall outside the warden's door. He doesn't know what to do. He stands there for a long, long, long time. Finally, he hears the warden calling.

Yes? says the guard, opening the door.

Hadley is lying on the floor.

The prisoner is sick, the warden says. You should probably take him to the infirmary.

The guard carries Hadley down the hall. Hadley coughs and coughs.

It's okay, says the guard. You're gonna be all right.

But he has a hard time believing what he says.

Hadley's eyes are swollen shut, and there are dark circles around them. His skin feels strange, and he is very cold.

How could this happen? thinks the guard.

The guard sits by Hadley's bed for days.

What's the matter with him, Doc? he keeps saying.

We don't really know, the doctor says. He's fine, except he's dying.

The guard looks at Hadley.

You can't fix him? he says.

No, says the doctor. We tried that. Best advice is hope and pray.

And then he walks away.

The guard stays in the infirmary every night. He holds Hadley's hand and talks to him.

Can you hear me, Hadley? he keeps saying. Can you hear me? I'm here. Can you hear me?

But the only response he ever gets is the sound of Hadley's shallow, ragged breathing. And then one day Hadley's cold and still, and the guard is all by himself.

The guard knocks on the warden's door. He does it with the butt of his gun.

Come in, says the warden, and the guard goes in.

What are you doing with that? says the warden.

What did you do to Hadley? says the guard.

What did I do? says the warden. I did nothing.

You did! yells the guard. He was fine until he saw you! You said something, you *did* something to him!

The warden stares at the guard. Then he shakes his head.

You wouldn't understand, he says.

I'll understand, the guard says. You'll make me.

And he raises and cocks the gun.

Go ahead and shoot, the warden says. You'll never learn anything from me. Go ahead, really; be my guest. It's not like it'll do you any good.

The guard's finger tightens on the trigger, but for some reason he can't seem to shoot. The trigger's stuck; something's wrong. He curses, tries again and again.

Meanwhile, the warden laughs.

When you're done, he says, you're fired. Turn in your gun on the way out. And your keys, your badge, and uniform.

The guard stands outside the prison gates. The other guard stands beside him.

I'm sorry, the other guard says to the guard. I don't know why things like this happen.

On the bus ride home, the guard sits quietly, staring out the window at the world. He watches dully as it all drifts by—all of it flat and gray. There is no sound but the sound of the engine, and the creaking of the worn-out bus. There are no other passengers on board. The guard is all by himself.

That night in bed, the guard stares at the ceiling, trying to get it all straight.

I'm no longer a guard, he thinks and thinks, over and over in his head.

He tries to see himself as something else, in some other line of work, but he can't think of a single job he would be qualified for.

In the end, all he sees is a man in his bed, lying there in the dark. Lying alone in the middle of the night.

What's the point? he says. What's the point.

The guard gets up. He goes to the closet. He opens it and finds an old uniform. He puts it on, takes a gun from the dresser, and then heads toward the door.

The guard walks the streets of the sleeping town. Everywhere, everything is deserted. Here and there, he seems to see a shadow—but the shadow is always of nothing.

Eventually the guard finds himself in the park that lies in the center of town. It's not much more than a patch of dirt and some sickly, broken trees. The guard stands staring up at the sky—at the cold, dark, empty sky—and as he does, a cloud takes the moon, and some dead leaves scrape on by.

The guard takes the gun out of its holster. He has owned this gun for years. He has fired it many, many times, but never for what you'd call real. He raises the gun and puts it to his head. He has never done anything like this. He has never even thought of doing such a thing. And yet here he is now, doing it. He feels the barrel against his skin. It feels cold; he can feel the roundness of the hole. He thinks of the bullet lying inside, waiting for its chance to be summoned out.

The guard's finger tightens on the gun's trigger and everything inside him starts to leap. And then he feels a touch on his arm—a hand, gentle, but firm.

The guard lowers the gun. He turns around, knowing full well what he'll see. And there, in the dark, he sees the face of the escaped dead prisoner, Hadley.

Please, says Hadley, hand over the gun.

The guard does so, without question.

You shouldn't be handling things like this, Hadley says. It just isn't safe.

The guard goes with Hadley back to the prison and they walk up and down the halls.

This was your cell, the guard says to Hadley.

Of course, says Hadley. There's the hole.

Hadley steps inside and kneels down, peers into the dark.

It's a long, long way, but not that far, he says, and he starts to crawl.

The guard stands and watches for a while, and then he looks around.

And in the morning when the warden appears, the prison is nowhere to be found.

APPENDIX

THE FOLLOWING IS A LONGER STORY
NOT PART OF THE SAME PROJECT
INCLUDED HERE AT THE PUBLISHER'S REQUEST

THE TV

ONE DAY THE MAN WAKES UP AND FINDS THAT HE DOES not feel like going to work. He is not sick, exactly; he just doesn't feel like going to work. He calls the office and makes an excuse, then he pours himself a bowl of cereal and sits down in front of the television.

The man doesn't usually have time to watch television, so it takes him a while to find a show he's interested in, but when he eventually does find it, he sits rapt, staring, his cereal forgotten, for a very, very, very long time. The show seems to last much longer than a normal show. In fact, it seems to last all day. It is five o'clock before the main character finally leaves his job and heads home, prompting the credits to roll.

The man sets his bowl of cereal aside and stares at the floor for a while.

My God, he thinks.

He gets up, goes into the bathroom, and gets into the shower. As he washes, he thinks about the show he has just seen. He is shampooing his hair when suddenly he realizes: the show was about him. Not kind of about him, not metaphorically about him, but actually *about him.*

That's why the main character looked so familiar, he thinks, dunking his head under the water.

But how could it have taken me so long to recognize my own self? he wonders. And how did they manage to find an actor who looks so exactly like me?

The man stays home from work again the next day, claiming to have the flu. The show is on again—his show. This time he watches it with his eyes open. Yep, there he is, arriving at work. He is wearing the suit he bought last week at Macy's. There he is, waving at the security guard he always waves at in the morning. Now he's walking down the hallway toward his office, now he's moving inside, there's his desk, his chair, his inbox and his outbox, his stapler and his letter opener. It's amazing; the man can hardly believe it. On-screen, he sits down at his desk, looks at the clock, and begins to work.

The man does the same thing at work every day; it is not very exciting. But somehow watching himself do it from inside his apartment, through the TV screen, is absolutely fascinating. The man is mesmerized by all the little unconscious movements his on-screen self makes. He seems to chew on his lip a lot.

Maybe that's why my lips are always chapped, he thinks, running a finger over them. He will have to watch that in the future.

At lunchtime, the man on-screen leaves the building and goes down the block to a little sandwich shop. It is Thursday, so the old man who owns the place is in. He and the man have a conversation about the state of the world while the man eats his sandwich (roast beef, same as always) and drinks his drink (coffee, black, same as always). Then the man returns to the office and works the rest of the day. At five o'clock he finishes up and heads out the door, and once again the credits roll.

This time the man on the couch studies the credits carefully. Yep, there's his name, listed both as the main character's and as that of the actor.

So it really *is* me, the man thinks in relief. It has been bothering him to think that an actor could so perfectly play him. It made him feel foolish to be so predictable, so reproducible. This way is much better. He feels proud of his role in the whole affair.

The next day, the man goes to work. He apologizes for having been absent for the past couple days, but no one seems to care very much. This does not surprise him, but still it seems a little sad. The man sits at his desk and does his work. It is not much fun. It has never been much fun, he reflects, but now it seems particularly burdensome. He spends most of the time trying not to chew on his lip, with little success. At lunch, he goes down to the corner store. It is Friday, so the old man who owns the place is not in, so the man sits alone at a table in the corner and remembers the conversation that his on-screen self had with the old man the day before. He smiles to himself about some of the witty and observant things the two of them said.

Something nice happens in the afternoon. The man discovers that because his on-screen self did his work so well over the past couple of days, he is now done for the week. The man can hardly believe it. He almost never finishes his full workload. Usually he has to stay late on Friday night, or even come in on Saturday or Sunday—or both—to get it all done. He sits at his desk, marveling for a long moment at the knowledge that he can go home early, and then he does. He waves good-bye to the security guard on his way out. He drives home feeling the wind in his hair and the sun on his face.

At home, the man turns on the TV and is surprised to find that his show is on. There he is, wearing the same clothes he is wearing right now, in real life—but he is *still at work*. He is sitting behind his desk, hunched over a legal pad, writing something.

But how can this be? the man thinks. All the work is finished! He squints at the TV, trying to see what exactly his other self is working on. It is hard to tell. He seems to be writing up a list of some kind.

The man notices that the man behind the desk is no longer chewing on his lip.

That night the program does not stop at five. The man in the office keeps right on working until almost nine-thirty. At home, the man has pulled a straight-backed chair up to the TV and sits staring, trying to figure out what's happening, what his other self is doing. He cannot figure it out. When the man finally finishes working on his list—or whatever it is he's working on—he slides it into his briefcase and leaves work for the day. Again. At home, the man sits with his eyes glued to the front door, waiting for himself to walk in. He has lots of questions. He wants to know what this list is all about. Ten, eleven, eleven-thirty, midnight. The door does not open.

Suddenly it occurs to the man that he can just open the briefcase and take out the list and read it. After all, it is *his* briefcase. He gets up and goes into the bedroom. Now, where did he put that briefcase? He can't remember. Where does he usually put it? He can't remember that, either. In fact, he suddenly realizes, he can't remember ever owning a briefcase at all.

The next day, the man awakens confused. He sits on the edge of the bed. He feels like he is forgetting something, but can't think what it could possibly be.

The man gets to the couch early so he won't miss anything. But he is surprised to find himself already seated behind the desk when he turns on the TV. There he is, with his feet up, reading a book. The book is lying open in his lap, so the man cannot tell what it is. It is very thick, though. There are other books stacked neatly nearby on the desk. The man squints to make out the titles, wondering what they're all about. Some of them seem to be about business management, but one is about calculus, and there are others about art and history, and one narrow volume seems to be a collection of poetry. The man smiles when he sees that. What on earth is going on?

When nine o'clock rolls around, the man behind the desk closes the book he's reading (is it the *dictionary*?) and gets down to work. He works quickly and with an air of extreme concentration. At home, the man on the couch, though filled with admiration for his other, better self, feels a twinge of jealousy, and even, strangely enough, something that feels like fear.

At lunch, the man on-screen does not go to the shop on the corner. Instead, he fixes his tie and then heads down the corridor in the direction of his boss's office. The man on the couch cannot believe what he's seeing. He watches as he knocks firmly on the boss's door and then goes inside, closing the door behind him and staying inside for some time. When he emerges fifteen minutes later, he is smiling. He stops and calls back to the person inside, something in the way of an affirmation, and then heads off along the hall, a spring in his step. With the remainder of his lunch hour, he eats a sandwich he has brought to work in a brown paper bag, and drinks a bottle of water.

The man at home does not know what's happening. He has never purposely gone to speak to his boss. In fact, he can't imagine ever wanting to do such a thing. Still, he admires his on-screen self for doing it. Perhaps something good will come of it—maybe a raise. The man goes into the kitchen and grabs a bag of cookies from the cupboard. But when he returns to the living room, he finds that his on-screen self has left early for the day. His office is clean, his outbox is full, his pile of books is gone.

The man sits staring at his empty office for some time. He begins to get antsy. Where has he gone? There is no way to know. What did he say to his boss? What was on the list? And what are all the books for? The man is beginning to feel nauseous thinking about it all. He is making himself sick. He has to think about something else. Perhaps there is something else on the television.

The man changes the channel. There is a cartoon about a coyote, a commercial for an exercise machine, someone talking about the weather, and, oh wait, what's this? There's the man again. He's in his car now, driving down a street with which the man on the couch is unfamiliar. He stops outside a building, an office building, and he goes inside. He speaks to a receptionist, and is then ushered into a conference room.

In the room are a number of men, all of whom look very serious. At home, the man on the couch is frightened. But his other self looks perfectly at ease. He places his briefcase carefully on the table, unlocks it with a pair of decisive clicks, and opens it up. Inside is a stack of papers. He begins to hand them out and, as he does so, he begins to speak. He speaks about things the man on the couch does not understand. Stocks and bonds and financial matters, things like that. The man on the couch furrows his brow, trying to follow it all. He can't, but he is relieved to see that the men in the room seem to be following it quite well and, what's more, seem to be quite happy with what they're hearing.

At the end of the meeting, the men rise, smiling, and spend quite some time congratulating the man on what he has said and done. Cigars are passed around and the man takes one and sees himself smoking it with a practiced air, despite the fact that he has never smoked a cigar before in his life, and wouldn't ever want to, as they are disgusting. Still, he has to admit, it is quite enjoyable.

When the man leaves the meeting, however, the show does not follow him. It stays in the conference room with the other men, and after a while—despite the fact that these other men are beginning to seem vaguely familiar—the man on the couch starts to tire of their banter. He figures he's probably gotten back to the office by now, so he changes the channel again.

He is almost back to his original station when suddenly he recognizes himself on a show about doctors. He is in surgery, raising his hands in the air as a nurse slips a pair of latex gloves over them. He almost didn't recognize himself, thanks to the mask that covers half his face, but there's no doubt about it, it's him—after all, if a man can't recognize himself, what *can* he recognize? This is his first day as a surgeon. Apparently the man has been going to night school. The man on the couch is impressed. He didn't know you could go to night school to become a surgeon, and yet it turns out that he himself has actually been doing it this whole time! He marvels at himself as he cuts open some poor man's chest and begins to operate on his malfunctioning heart. He hopes the operation will go well, and it does. The nurses congratulate him as he sews the man back together. Later on they all go out drinking and the man makes love to one of the nurses—the more attractive one—in the bathroom of the club. It is the best sex the man has had in years.

On another station, the man finds himself foiling a gang of jewel thieves. He has infiltrated the gang thanks to some ingenious plastic surgery and a number of carefully constructed lies. He waits until the last possible moment and then he springs the trap. Everyone is arrested and found guilty and after the trial the man is singled out for bravery and is given a medal and a monument is erected to him in a park downtown. Lovers sit on a bench beside the monument and feel safe. Still, it is sad because the man's father once died in a botched robbery, and while what the man has done makes himself feel better, as though he has finally evened out the situation, he knows that nothing he can do will ever bring his father back from the dead. Still, though, perhaps his work has prevented other innocent fathers from being killed.

Meanwhile, the man is a scientist who has invented a way to bring people back from the dead. He uses it to bring back his wife, who died a few years ago, but then he learns that she didn't love him after all and that it is better not to mess with bringing people back from the dead. He is a better man for learning this, but still he can't help but feel sorry for himself, as he misses his wife and the love that he thought she had for him. On another station, the man is punching another man—himself?—in the face over and over again. The man sees the glory and the horror in this, but he doesn't feel like watching it right now. On another station the man has become the head of a warlike country and is threatening to unleash Armageddon on the world if his barbarous demands are not met. The man becomes afraid of himself and changes the channel. Now he is murdering a small boy in a field with a rusty knife and he feels absolutely terrible. Whatever happened to night school and books about poetry? He changes the channel again. There he is, trying to sell himself some kind of cleaning product. And now he is running down the street faster than an airplane thanks to the wonderful shoes he has invented, and blackmailing a political figure even though he himself is not without sin. The man is beginning to become confused. He is proud of himself and everything he has accomplished, very proud indeed—he always knew he had it in him. But at the same time he is scared of what he sees. There are things about himself that he doesn't want to know, things he does that he doesn't want to think about. He wishes there were some way he could choose what he does and does not do. But it is beyond his control. He runs rampant across the world, helping and killing and saving and selling, buying and raping and stealing and feeling and making love and running away and laughing and crying and dying and being born and dying and being born and dying and being born and dying and being born. The man cannot take it anymore, he can't take it anymore. He walks into the other room and puts a shotgun in his mouth and just then the show comes abruptly to an end.

Eventually the man comes to see that he has a mind, and that his mind is like a fist, wrapped tightly around a single thought. He cannot open the fist to look at the thought, for fear that it will fly away, but he knows that it is very important and that he must hang on to it, no matter the cost. He stares at the fist and hopes that it is very strong. He feels like a man who has fallen asleep at the wheel and has awakened to find his car lurching off a cliff. He has applied the brake, he has swung the wheel to the side, he has offered up a silent prayer, but it is as yet too soon to see whether he has done these things in time. He can only wait for the next moment to come, and hope as hard as he can.

Finally the next moment comes. The man realizes that the thing in his hand is not a thought but the end of an electrical cord. He looks down and finds that the electrical cord leads to the television—now a dark, silent box lying on the floor at his feet. The man feels a rush of triumph. He has come out on top, he has won. He grins to himself as he contemplates his next move. He decides that the best thing to do is to take the TV down to the trash and get rid of it. And this is exactly what he does.

But in the stairwell on the way back from the trash, the man passes himself carrying the television down to the trash. He stops to congratulate himself on his wisdom and strength, but his other self averts his eyes, hoping not to be noticed. The man begins to take offense and is about to say something, when both of them are elbowed aside by a third version of the man who is carrying his TV back up from the trash. The man hurries after himself, yelling No, No, I don't want that anymore! but he doesn't listen. As they enter the apartment, the man on the couch looks up from the TV in irritation. Why can't everyone leave him alone? The room is packed with versions of the man, running here and there, talking to himself about this and that, making plans on the phone and staring out the window and falling in love and falling out of love and finding himself loved and unloved and hated and feared and liked and disliked and ignored and unknown and known. He is fired, promoted, re-hired, and refired, has found a new place to live and is moving out, is moving in and repainting, is in the other room dying and in the kitchen being born. There is too much going on. The man walks out the door and down the hall and into the next apartment. Mommy, Mommy, scream his children, what's for breakfast? The man makes French toast and waffles and ham and eggs and pancakes and cereal and Pop-Tarts and brownies and hot dogs and hamburgers and Baked Alaska and a birthday cake in the shape of a castle and pours glasses of milk and orange juice and coffee and Tang and Kool-Aid and water and puts ice in all the glasses, trying to ignore himself as he murders each and every one of the kids over and over and over again in hundreds of different ways and gets a job in another country under an assumed name and pees all over the dining room floor and draws on the wall in crayon. He takes the kids down to the bus stop seven hundred times and he drives the bus to school—drunk, sober, hungover, on acid, pot, cocaine, uppers and downers, or nothing at all—it doesn't matter in the least, he gets in an accident every foot of the way, or he doesn't. At school, he gets in a fight on the playground and is sent to the office, or doesn't and isn't, or does and isn't, or doesn't and is. He gives himself a good lecture, maybe, winks at the secretary he has or has not been banging for the past two weeks, or four weeks, or ten weeks, or no weeks, then hurries slowly to the women's room, realizing that it is or is not his time of the month, mops none or half or all of the gym, and goes out back to have a smoke or stare at the sky or remember the time he accidentally ate a spider or became president or something else or nothing else or everything else. He flies to the next town over and perches in all the trees, then falls to the ground in several different countries and is blown away by the wind, which hammers endlessly in all the ears he has—more than he is capable of counting—for approximately 93 billion years, as good a guess as any to a time outside of time.

The man especially loves it when he is a doctor, a lawyer, a caveman, a cowboy, an old man who owns a luncheonette and talks to the people who come in to eat every day. He hates it when he is a doctor, a lawyer, a caveman, a cowboy, an old man who owns a luncheonette and talks to the people who come in to eat every day, but he loves it when he is a comedian, a beautiful young model, an astronaut, the king of England, a profiler working for the Federal Bureau of Investigation. It is very exciting. He loves to taunt the profiler by sending him long, cryptic notes written in human blood. He knows he will never catch him, and even if he does, it doesn't really matter because he is already dead and buried and being eaten by worms and will probably just get another medal and a raise anyway.

Sometimes the man cries himself to sleep at night, but usually he just changes the channel. He has not been able to find his way to the office; he doesn't know where they put it. He rings and rings, but the nurse no longer answers his calls. One night he discovers that his lips are horribly chapped. This strikes him as the worst thing that has ever happened, and he sobs uncontrollably for almost fourteen seconds. Then, once more, he opens the fist.

ACKNOWLEDGMENTS

The stories in this book grew out of a class I took in horror writing taught by Dennis Etchison at the Mystery and Imagination Bookshop in Glendale, California (owned and operated by Christine and Malcolm Bell).

The stories were edited by my friend Maureen de Sousa; my mother, Barbara Loory; and my editor (and personal savior) Josh Kendall at Penguin Books.

This book would not exist without the support of Willing Davidson at *The New Yorker* and the strange and miraculous prestidigitation of my friend and agent Sarah Funke Butler.

The following people provided invaluable assistance as readers and listeners and thinker-throughers: above all, my screenwriting partner Andra Moldav (to whom I owe solutions to many conundrums), Aaron Dietz, Alex Reed, Andrew Ramer, Anna Dale, Bonnie Thompson, Brad Listi, Brian Doucet, Brian Travis, Brian Wright, Carl Harders, Charlotte Howard, Chrissy Wasserman, Claudia Barria, Desi Fish, Duke Haney, Gina Rho, Grant Story,

Heather Conley, Irene Zion, Jack Long, Jack Zipes, James Othmer, Jason Vincz, Jenieke Allen, Jennifer Guinn, Jennifer Peltz, Jennifer Weaver-Jones, Jeremy Tolbert, Jodi Kaplan and Mike Lester, Jonathan Evison, Keith Dixon, Kelci M. Kelci, Lara Loory, Lauren Becker, Lenore Zion, Lindsay Foose, Loomis Fall, Lora Grillo, Maggie Riggs, Maggie Tiojakin, Mark Krieger, Margaret Walsh, Martyn Conterio, Mary Guterson, Matt Comito, Michael Armida, Mike Armstrong, Moses Robinson, Nina Kuruvilla, Patty Gates, Roxane Gay, Scott Garson, Stacey Kirkland, Stephanie Warren, Steve Himmer, and Trish Bash.

Thanks to my family and friends who kept me sane, all the editors who printed my stories, the members of Soda & His Million Piece Band, The Peculiar Pretzelmen, *The Nervous Breakdown,* and the Fiction Files.

This book was written exclusively to *Alina* by Arvo Pärt.

Happy Birthday, Megan Nico DiLullo!